DO NOT REMOVE
CARDS FROM POCKET

The Long Way Home

by Barbara Cohen

illustrated by Diane de Groat

Lothrop, Lee & Shepard Books
New York

Text copyright © 1990 by Barbara Cohen
Illustrations copyright © 1990 by Diane de Groat

First Edition   1 2 3 4 5 6 7 8 9 10

Library of Congress Cataloging in Publication Data
Cohen, Barbara. The long way home / by Barbara Cohen; illustrated by Diane de Groat.
    p.   cm. Summary: Sally's relationship with an elderly bus driver who recites Shakespeare stories helps her to cope with the problems of her mother's cancer and being separated from her twin sister at summer camp. ISBN 0-688-09674-3 [1. Cancer—Fiction. 2. Twins—Fiction. 3. Camps—Fiction.] I. De Groat, Diane, ill. II. Title. PZ7.C6595Lm 1990 [Fic]—dc20
                        89-35309 CIP AC

For Sara and Cecil

O N E

"**M**om is throwing up again," Emily announced.

Sally looked up from her book. "How do you know?"

"I listened at the bathroom door. I could hear her." Emily put her hand on her throat. "You know—aargh, aargh."

"Our bathroom?" Sally said. "She's throwing up in our bathroom?"

Emily nodded.

"I wonder why she always uses our bathroom when she has to throw up. She has a perfectly good bathroom of her own."

"Maybe she doesn't want to stink it up for Dad," Emily suggested.

"But it's okay to stink it up for you and me and Lisa."

"Oh, Sally!" Emily sat down on the bed next to her twin. "You know she isn't throwing up because she wants to throw up."

"Yeah, I know," Sally said. "Of course I know. I'm sorry." She couldn't understand herself. Right now she should be kinder and more loving to her mother than ever. Instead, she found herself actually hating her some of the time. She slid off her bed and stared at herself in the full-length mirror that hung on the closet door. She put her hand behind her back and pulled her T-shirt tight, so that she could see her emerging breasts pushing against the fabric. "What do you think, Emily? When we're Mother's age, do you think we'll get breast cancer, too? I read somewhere that it's hereditary."

"I'm not going to worry about that now," Emily replied. "I don't even *have* breasts yet."

She didn't. Emily and Sally were fraternal twins, not identical—no more alike in appearance or personality than any other pair of sisters. Before she got sick, Mom had said, "Sally, I've got to buy you training bras."

"How about me?" Emily had interjected immediately.

"You don't need them yet," Mom replied.

"Get her some, anyway," Sally said. "They won't hurt her, will they?"

"No, I suppose not." Mother laughed. "Sally, you won't wear what Emily *isn't* wearing, and Emily, you have to wear whatever Sally *is* wearing."

"Not if it doesn't look good on me," Emily said. "I never borrow her green sweater. You put green on me, I look like I've got a bad case of creeping crud."

"No one sees a bra," Sally explained seriously.

"You don't say!" Mom returned. And then they all laughed.

Sally thought maybe that was the last time they'd giggled together. Soon after, the doctor found the lump in their mother's breast. No one had taken Sally shopping for bras, and Emily's chest remained as thin and flat as a sheet of plywood. Emily was lucky. Sally hadn't thought so three months ago, but she thought so now.

Emily opened a drawer and pulled out a pair of shorts and a clean T-shirt. "Come on, Sally," she said. "You'd better get dressed. That van will be here to pick us up in half an hour."

"I don't want to go," Sally said.

"Who wants to go?" Emily returned. "But what are we going to do—sit around the house for the rest of the summer and watch Mom vomit?"

"Emily!"

"I know. I'm sorry."

In the space of five minutes, they'd both been sorry. That was too many sorrys for one morning. Silently they dressed and went downstairs. Dad had already left for work. Lisa was gulping down a glass of orange juice. Mom, still in her robe, sat at the kitchen table, sipping tea and chewing on saltines. She didn't look too bad. Her hair had thinned some, but it hadn't fallen out; she didn't have to wear a wig.

Lisa kissed Mom's cheek. "I have to go to the Gregorys now. Mrs. Gregory is going out early today."

Sally thought it would be wonderful to be fourteen and earn fifty dollars a week baby-sitting, the way Lisa did. But not baby-sitting the Gregory kids. They were horrid. She wouldn't take care of them for a thousand dollars a week.

"Will you be all right, Mom?" Lisa asked.

"Of course," Mom said. She rose to her feet and hugged Lisa. "Have a good day, honey." Lisa picked up her beach bag and left the house. Mom turned to the twins. "What do you want for breakfast? Cereal? Eggs?"

"Sit down, Mom," Emily ordered. "It's too hot for eggs. We'll have cereal, and we can get it for ourselves."

I want eggs, Sally thought. I want my mother to make me eggs. But she didn't say it out loud.

Of the two of them, Emily had always been the fresh twin, the mischievous twin, the rebellious twin. She used to tease her sister sometimes, calling her "Saint Sally." But somehow, not so very long ago, Emily had turned into the good twin. Sally couldn't imagine how it had happened.

Now Sally wanted her mother to say "Don't be silly, girls. I'll get your breakfast." But she didn't; she only sank gratefully back into her chair.

Emily plopped a box of Frosted Flakes, two bananas, and some milk on the table. "Did you pack lunches for us?" Sally asked as she dribbled a little cereal into a bowl. She actually hated Frosted Flakes, but she didn't have the energy to get up and take a different cereal. Fortunately, she liked bananas.

"Dad did, last night," Mother said.

"Dad doesn't make very good lunches," Sally said.

Mother didn't say anything.

"I don't know why we have to go to this camp, anyway," Sally continued. "We could have gone to the shore with Jenny and Jake. Aunt Lou and Uncle Andrew would have taken us, too."

"We've gone over this five thousand times," Mom said with a sigh. "I could not impose three extra children on my sister. Where would you all have slept?"

"On the floor, in sleeping bags," Sally said. Every summer for as long as she could remember, her family and her aunt's family had spent the month of August on Long Beach Island in two cottages located side by side. But this year, because Mother had to get chemotherapy treatments, they weren't going. Emily and Sally wouldn't be rafting in the surf this summer; they wouldn't be riding their bikes to the lighthouse; they wouldn't be crabbing in the bay; they wouldn't be making sand castings out of messy mixes of plaster of paris and seawater. Jenny and Jake would be doing all those things without them.

"On the floor for a month?" her mother replied. "Don't be ridiculous, Sally."

"I wouldn't want to leave you, anyway," Emily said, patting her mother's hand.

Sally thought *she* was going to vomit. Instead she chewed hard on a piece of banana. "I hope it rains every day for the whole month," she said.

"You don't mean that," said Mom.

"Yes, I do," Sally insisted.

"You won't have much fun at day camp if it rains every day."

"I won't have any fun there, anyway." Suddenly the anger drained from her voice. "Please, Mom, please, let me stay home. I'll read, I'll watch TV, I'll make my own lunch. You won't even know I'm here."

"I know. That's what you've done since school let out."

No, Sally protested inwardly. That's what you

thought I was doing. What I was actually doing was worrying.

Mom picked up a saltine and put it down again. "You'd be perfectly content to spend the entire summer in the house. But summer is the time to be outside, in the air, doing things."

"Doing things *at the beach.*"

"That is enough, Sally." Mom pushed herself away from the table and headed for the bathroom. "I don't want to hear another word about it."

"Look what you've done," Emily hissed. "You've made her sick again."

"I did not make her sick," Sally hissed back. "That dumb chemotherapy makes her sick."

Outside a horn blew, penetrating the walls of the house with sharp insistence. "The van," Emily said. "Come on, let's go." They took their lunch boxes out of the refrigerator, shoved them into their knapsacks, and hurried toward the door. "Bye, Mom," Emily shouted as she passed the powder room. Sally didn't say anything.

"Bye, darlings," Mom managed to shout back. "Have a good day."

How can we have a good day? Sally thought. How can we have a good day when we're leaving you in the bathroom, retching out your guts? Have a good day, indeed. Sally was sure she'd never have a good day again.

Nothing happened to change her opinion. The van driver was a perfect ditz. "Are you the Bergs?" she asked as they climbed on the van.

"Who else?" Sally retorted.

"Your house is hard to find."

"It is?" No one had ever said that before. The number, 459, was clearly visible next to the door, and Bittersweet Drive was right in the middle of Watch Mountain.

"Well, anyway, I found it." The driver ran her hand through her short white hair, and it stood up straight, as if she'd electrocuted herself. "I'm Claire. Who are you?"

"I'm Emily," Emily said. "This is Sally."

"Sit down, guys. Make yourselves comfortable. It's going to be a long trip."

It was. They were the first ones to be picked up. Though she had the names and addresses of all the campers on a list, and a county map with her route marked in red ink, Claire managed to get lost finding every single house. "Geez," Sally whispered, "if the swimming counselor is like her, we'll all drown."

Emily giggled, and then, as the van pulled up in front of a brick condominium, she shouted, "Hey, I know who lives here."

"You do?" asked Claire. "Who?"

"Gloria Blake."

Claire peered at her list. "That's right!" Again she ran her fingers through her hair, as if she were amazed at this incredibly lucky coincidence. "Thank goodness." She blew the horn. Gloria opened the door and hurried down the walk. Her best friend, Petey Haberman, was with her.

"You're late," Petey said as she climbed on the van.

"This house was very hard to find," Claire explained.

"My house hard to find?" Gloria returned. "No one ever said that before."

"You must be Gloria, then. I'm Claire." She turned to Petey. "Who are you?"

"Petey Haberman."

Claire examined the list once again. "Marvelous! One less house to find. Go ahead, sit."

Emily stood up and waved. "Petey, Gloria, here." They took seats in front of Emily and Sally. "I didn't know you were coming to Camp Totem, too. This is wonderful."

"We didn't know, either, until a couple of days ago," Petey said. "I'm sorry, we should have called you."

"What's the matter?" said Sally. "Are your mothers sick, too?"

"What do you mean, sick?" said Gloria. Then she remembered. "Oh, you mean like your mom. No, but they work. We always went to the Y camp, but this year, at the last minute they decided we're too old for the Y camp. They decided we needed a more advanced program. They heard Camp Totem is excellent."

"We'll never know," Sally said, "unless we get there." Actually, though she wasn't jumping up and down like Emily, she was just as glad that Petey and Gloria would be with them at camp. She and Emily hung out with Petey and Gloria all the time at school. Fooling around with them on the van made the trip seem slightly less than endless. They'd been picked up at eight-thirty. It was ten o'clock before they drove through the wooden arch that marked the entrance to the camp.

A counselor met them in the parking lot. "Claire, what happened?" he asked.

"Those houses were very hard to find," Claire said.

"Well, it was the first morning. The route will go much faster tomorrow, I'm sure."

"I'm not," Sally murmured.

The counselor, who introduced himself as Gerald, called their names and told them which group they'd be in. Emily, Petey, and Gloria were Senecas. Sally was an Apache. She had no idea why she'd been separated from everyone she knew and sent off to spend the day with a bunch of strangers. When she mentioned it to Gerald, he said, "They probably broke up you and your twin on purpose."

"Well, then, couldn't you let either Gloria or Petey be an Apache, too?"

"I'm sorry, kid, but I can't," he said. "Ruth made up the tribes. I can't fool around with them. It would throw everything off."

"Who's Ruth?"

"She's the head counselor. She's the boss."

It wasn't fair, Sally thought. She was the only Apache on the van. All the others were Senecas or Seminoles or Pawnees. Gerald was the Apache counselor, so he led Sally up a hill to a large tent that, he explained, was the Apache headquarters. Sally turned around and watched her sister and her friends disappear into the woods on the other side of the parking lot. She didn't see them again all day.

The Apaches played volleyball, they had a treasure hunt, they ate lunch, they started weaving belts out of leather strips, and they swam. A man named Cliff Breakwater, who claimed to be a real Native American, took them on a nature walk through the woods. Afterward they sat around and listened to Gerald tell about some of the things that were going to happen during the rest of the month. "At the end," he said, "there'll be a big powwow. All the tribes will gather at a campfire and they'll each have to do something. We've got to start thinking now about what we're going to do. We have to plan something really spectacular if we want to win."

"What do you get if you win?" Sally asked.

"It's an honor to win," said Gerald. "An honor to the tribe. Your tribe's name and the year get inscribed on a plaque in the office."

Sally picked a blade of grass and sucked on it to keep herself from answering Gerald with a fresh remark. Was she turning into Emily, and was Emily turning into her? Maybe that was why she was here, all alone among the Apaches. Maybe it was a punishment.

At last it was time to leave. When she boarded the van, Sally was so glad to see Emily that she almost kissed her. She almost kissed Petey and Gloria, too. But the three of them were too busy chattering about life among the Senecas to notice that she'd taken her seat beside Emily. "Coopy Palmer's cute," Petey said. "Really cute. I think he'll be my boyfriend."

"He's not as cute as Claudio," said Emily.

"You can have Claudio for your boyfriend."

"Don't you think we're a little young for boyfriends?" Gloria asked.

"I'm almost eleven," Petey said. "You already are. We're going into sixth grade. Some people have boyfriends in fifth grade. Like Stacey and Joe last year."

"That was all Stacey's idea," Sally chimed in. "I don't think Joe had a thing to do with it."

Suddenly they realized she was there. "Was there anyone cute in your tribe?" Emily asked.

"Not only wasn't there anyone cute, there was no one you could even talk to," Sally snapped. "The minute Gerald turned his back, they started throwing stuff at each other—pieces of leather, sand, volley-balls—whatever they could get their hands on. That's their idea of fun. He knew it was going on, and he didn't do a thing about it. He was too busy standing on the path flirting with that Seminole counselor."

"Amy," Gloria said.

"Yeah, Amy. She doesn't look any better to me than all those dumb Apaches."

"Most of the Senecas are nice," Gloria said.

"At least so far," Emily added.

"Tomorrow I'm going to ask Ruth to transfer me to the Senecas," said Sally. "And if she doesn't, I'm not going back."

"You have to come back," Emily insisted.

"No, I don't." Sally leaned her head against the back of her seat, folded her arms across her chest, and shut her eyes. She shut her ears, too. She didn't want to hear any more about all the fun the Senecas had had that day.

The sound of Emily shouting startled her eyes open. "Hey, Claire," Emily called out. "Where are we?"

Sally clutched Emily's arm. "What's the matter?"

Emily glanced at her watch. "We've been driving around for half an hour, and we haven't dropped off a single kid."

"I guess we're lost again," Claire said. She didn't sound in the least upset.

"*We're* not lost," Sally muttered. "*You're* lost."

"What's the difference?" Emily said, and sighed.

Claire was still talking. "But don't worry about it. You'll all get home eventually."

"If we don't die of starvation first," said Sally. She rummaged in her lunch box, hoping for a sliver of carrot, a crust of bread. She found nothing but a dirty paper napkin and some crumpled plastic wrap.

"And in the meantime," Claire continued, "I'll tell you a story."

One of the boys in the backseat called out, "We're not three years old."

"You don't have to listen," Claire said.

But it was hard not to listen. Claire's voice, like her electric white hair, was something Sally couldn't ignore. Rich and melodic, it easily rose above the rattle of the van and the shouts and sneers of the kids. And after a while, they shut up and listened. Sally discovered she wanted to listen, too. She became totally absorbed in the story.

T W O

"Once upon a time," Claire began, "there was a pair of twins."

Emily and Sally looked at each other. Twins. They hadn't read many stories about twins.

"A girl named Viola and a boy named Sebastian."

Emily and Sally looked at each other again. Fraternal twins. They had read even fewer stories about fraternal twins.

Claire went on with the story. The twins were shipwrecked and landed in a country called Illyria. But they were separated, and each feared the other was dead. Viola disguised herself as a boy and went to work for Duke Orsino, with whom she immediately fell in love. But he was in love with the Countess Olivia. He sent Viola, now called Cesario, to

Olivia's house with love messages, and bang, Olivia immediately fell in love with her! Or was it him? Even Viola/Cesario didn't seem quite sure.

Olivia had an uncle, Sir Toby Belch, who wanted her to marry his friend, Sir Andrew Aguecheek. Olivia had a steward, too, named Malvolio, whom no one could stand. Malvolio was so vain that he thought Olivia was in love with him.

With so many characters in love with the wrong person, the story was extremely confusing. It became even more confusing as it went on, because, of course, eventually Sebastian showed up, and all those lovesick characters kept taking Viola/Cesario for Sebastian, and Sebastian for Viola/Cesario. Eventually, Viola managed to straighten out the entire mess, and the story ended with lots of singing and dancing and just about everyone in sight getting married.

"Well," asked Claire when she was done, "what did you think?" At last, she had found her way to one of the camper's houses and pulled the van up to the curb.

Sally reached out and put her hand on Claire's shoulder. "That was probably the silliest story I ever heard," she said. "Where did you get such a silly story?"

"It's a play by William Shakespeare. It's called *Twelfth Night*. He wrote it almost four hundred years ago; maybe that's why you didn't like it." Claire sounded rather disappointed.

"I didn't say I didn't like it," Sally explained quickly. "I just said it was silly. A person can like silly things. Pee-Wee Herman is very silly; I like him."

Claire brightened immediately. "Oh, good. Tomorrow, if we get lost, I'll tell you another."

"I hope we don't get lost."

"Don't count it."

"Listen," Sally said, "do you want to know why it's such a silly story?" She didn't wait for an answer. "They weren't identical twins. They couldn't be, because Viola was a girl and Sebastian was a boy. So no one would ever really mix them up, no matter how much alike they were dressed."

"Did Viola and Sebastian and all the others make you forget your troubles, for just a little while?" Claire asked.

"Well . . . sort of," Sally admitted. Claire's question had surprised her. Claire knew kids could have troubles. Most grown-ups had forgotten that.

"That's all that matters," Claire said. "It's just a story. That's one of the things stories are for, maybe the main thing. Now, lean back. We've got to get rolling again."

Sally settled back in her seat. Petey, Gloria, and Emily were busy chattering, but Sally wasn't interested in tuning them in. She was thinking about Shakespeare. She knew who he was—the greatest poet and playwright in the English language. They'd learned that in fifth grade during the unit on Great Britain, but she'd heard of Shakespeare before then. Her mother had studied Shakespeare in college and had an enormous volume of his complete works illustrated with full-page colored paintings, one for each play. Sally and Emily had loved to look at those pictures when they were little—the people were dressed in such strange and beautiful clothes, more beautiful even than the knights and princesses in the fairy-tale book.

Claire told them no more stories that afternoon, and she didn't get lost again, either. In a matter of minutes, Sally and Emily were dropped in front of their house.

Mother was dozing on the living-room couch, but she woke up when the girls came in. "Well, how did it go?" she asked.

"Not so bad," said Emily.

"Awful," said Sally.

Though they spoke at the same time, their mother answered them separately. "First, the bad news," she said to Sally. "Then, the good news, Emily."

"Emily and I were separated," Sally said. "I didn't even get to be with Petey or Gloria. I'm in this tribe where I don't know one single kid, and they're all jerks."

"How can you be sure they're jerks if you don't know them?" Mother wondered.

"I can tell," Sally remarked darkly. She sat down

on the end of the couch. Her mother pulled her feet up just in time. "And then we have the dumbest van driver in the universe. She gets lost every other minute. Did you ever hear of a driver who can't read a map? I mean, doesn't a driver have to pass a test or something?" She didn't mention that Claire knew good stories. She didn't mention that Claire knew kids had troubles.

Emily's day sounded a lot better, full of interesting new friends and one or two activities she almost admitted enjoying. "What about you, Mom?" she asked. "How was your day?"

"Oh, not bad. I'll probably feel pretty good by Wednesday or Thursday."

"Until you have to go for another chemotherapy treatment," said Sally.

"That's not until a week from Friday. That'll be treatment number five. After that, just fifteen more to go." She sighed. "I'm lucky, really. I only have to stay on it for six months. Some people have to stay on it for a year, two years even."

"Lucky?" said Sally. "Lucky? Lucky would be not getting cancer at all."

"People get things," Mother said. "That's life. Sooner or later, everyone gets something."

"You could have gotten a cold," Sally said. "Or maybe pneumonia. You could have broken your arm. You're too young to have cancer."

"Even a kid can get cancer," Emily said. "Remember Arletta Miller? She died of leukemia when she was only in second grade. That's a kind of cancer. Blood cancer."

"Thanks, Emily," Sally retorted. "That's just what we wanted to hear." She picked up her knapsack and hurried out of the room. She thought maybe she was going to cry, and Mother didn't need to see that.

They weren't quite as late getting to Camp Totem on Tuesday as they'd been on Monday, but they were late. Claire had gotten lost again, but not lost enough to tell any stories. Sally was almost sorry. She wouldn't have minded another story as silly as *Twelfth Night*. This time, no one was waiting for them in the parking lot.

"I think I'll just go with you," Sally told Emily. "Probably no one will notice."

"Well, okay—I guess," said Emily.

Sally felt as if she'd touched a live electric wire. "Don't you *want* me to come with you? This is the first time they've ever separated us. I don't like it, but maybe you do." She turned away and started across the parking lot.

Emily ran after her and grabbed her arm. "Sally, listen. Let me explain."

Sally stood still. "Go ahead, explain."

"You know they'd have separated us at school if

Watch Mountain weren't so small that there's only one class for each grade. You know that's true. They always seat us on opposite sides of the room. They'd have separated us at Hebrew school, too, if Mom hadn't objected to carpooling four days a week instead of two. It's probably good for us to be separated now and then. Not all the time. Just once in a while. Besides," she added without a pause, "our counselor wouldn't let you stay with the Senecas. She has a list."

"I understand," Sally said through clenched teeth. "I understand perfectly."

"You don't understand at all," said Emily.

Sally turned away again and started up the hill. When she reached the Apache tent at the top, she turned and looked back. Emily was gone.

The Apaches were seated in a circle outside the tent. "Claire get lost again?" Gerald asked when he saw Sally.

"Yes," Sally said. "Why doesn't the camp fire her and hire a van driver who knows how to drive?"

"Oh, Claire's a safe driver," Gerald said. "She'll catch on to the route in a day or two. I think she needs the job."

"Would you want an unemployed carpenter to do surgery on you just because he needed the job?" Sally returned sharply.

A girl laughed. Sally glanced behind her to see who

she was—a pretty girl with long black hair and smooth olive skin against which her teeth gleamed so white she could have posed for a toothpaste ad. She hadn't been there yesterday.

"Sally, meet Melanie," said Gerald. "She started today. We have a new boy, too." The new boy was sitting next to Melanie. He told the group his name was Marty. He was as fair as Melanie was dark, but equally good-looking, with a headful of honey-colored short-cropped curls and a sprinkling of freckles across his nose. When he spoke, Sally detected a midwestern twang in his voice. A little space separated him from the next kid in the circle, and it was there that Sally decided to sit.

Cliff Breakwater was in the middle of the circle, showing them how Indians made fire without matches. The kids seemed to be paying attention, maybe because Cliff was clearly a no-nonsense type. If you threw sand at him, he'd throw it right back at you and get you in the eye, for sure.

When Cliff told them to form into groups of three or four, Sally felt panic rise up in her throat. She was sure to be one of those leftover kids the adult in charge had to assign to a group. But then, Melanie leaned across Marty. "Do you want to be with me?" she asked.

"Sure," said Sally. "Thanks."

"Hey, how about me?" asked Marty.

"Oh, you, too, naturally," Melanie said. "We have to have three."

They were supposed to try to make fire the way Cliff had, with two sticks, a leather thong, and a handful of dry leaves and twigs. They struggled for half an hour without producing so much as a single spark. All around them little fires crackled. The successful groups were toasting marshmallows that Cliff had given them.

"I just wasn't cut out to be an Indian," Sally said. "Whoever heard of a Jewish Indian, anyway?"

Melanie laughed.

"I'm from Ohio and my great-grandmother came from North Dakota," Marty said. "Maybe I have some Indian blood in me someplace, but I still can't get this fire started."

"Indians today use matches," Sally said. "I'm sure of that."

Cliff appeared and bent down to examine their futile efforts. "We're working very hard," said Sally. "It isn't our fault we're not getting anywhere. You should give us some marshmallows for trying."

"If it isn't your fault," Cliff asked, "whose fault is it?"

"There's something wrong with these sticks. Or these leaves. Maybe they got wet."

Cliff twirled the sticks several times. Sparks flew into the leaves. He cupped his hands around them and blew on them gently, fanning them into a tiny flame. "See?" he said. "Nothing wrong with the leaves or the sticks." Then he stamped the fire out.

"Oh, no," Marty exclaimed. "Don't do that."

Cliff handed the sticks to Marty. "Try again," he said. "Imagine it's the middle of winter, you're lost on a windswept plain, and if you don't get a fire going, you'll die." He walked off, carrying his sack of marshmallows with him. It was time for him to show some other lucky tribe how to build a fire. He taught nature and Indian lore to the whole camp.

"I think I hate this place. I'd rather be on that windswept plain, even without a fire," Sally said. Marty and Melanie laughed. "You think that was funny?" she asked.

They both nodded. Sally shrugged. She'd never considered herself a wit. No one else she knew did, either. Maybe it was a good thing to meet some new kids once in a while.

Marty bent over the pile of leaves.

"Hey, jerko, don't you know you'll burn your ugly mug if you get too close?" Sally looked up. A tall, skinny kid was standing behind Marty. Two other boys were with him, sucking marshmallows.

"Not a chance," said the fat one. "He'll never get that fire started."

"Go on, get out of here," Marty said. "Mind your own business."

"You are our business," the tall one said. "It's guys like you who mess up this whole tribe."

Sally recognized the threesome from the day before. The skinny one was Angelo; his sidekicks were named Maxie and Gil. "It's guys like *you* who mess up the whole tribe," she said, "throwing sticks and sand around when no one's looking, like three-year-olds."

"Watch out, smart mouth," said Gil. "We can take care of you."

"I'm scared," Sally said. "Real scared."

The rest of the Apaches went swimming. Sally, Marty, and Melanie had to stay behind, struggling on with their two sticks and their pile of leaves. By the time the other kids returned from the lake, they found the three of them sitting around their fire, toasting the marshmallows with which Cliff had at last stopped by to reward them. "Hey," Gerald said, "good for you. Three cheers for Sally, Marty, and Melanie."

"Three cheers?" Angelo said. "Three cheers? They're going to mess us up. We'll never win the powwow if we're stuck with the three of them."

Sally noticed several nods of grim agreement.

"Making a fire is just one thing," Marty announced calmly.

"Anyway, who says making fires is what we're going to do at the powwow? You don't know how good we may be at some things you won't be able to do at all."

"I won't hold my breath," Angelo said.

Marty shrugged and walked away. Sally and Melanie followed him. "Who cares about any old powwow," Sally said. "What's a powwow, anyway? I think we're too old for that kind of stuff. Have you noticed that the Senecas and the Apaches are the oldest tribes here? Compared to the little kid tribes, we're really small."

"I think Angelo and Gil were here first session," Marty said. "No wonder they have no trouble making fires."

"So what are we doing in this place, anyway?" Melanie wondered.

"I'm here because my mom's sick and we couldn't go to the shore," said Sally.

"I'm here because my dad lost his job," said Marty. "My folks can't afford to send me to sleep-away camp on Mom's salary."

"I don't know why I'm here," said Melanie. "I'm just here."

Hands in the pockets of his jeans, Marty leaned against an oak tree. "I'm not going to worry about that powwow. I'm just going to try to have some fun."

"Well," Sally returned drily, "lots of luck."

———

In the van going home, Emily asked Sally, "Was it so bad today?" Sally didn't answer right away. Emily gazed at her intently. "Well," she said at last, "are you going to tell me or not?"

"It's not such an easy question to answer," Sally said. She had never lied to Emily; she wasn't going to start now. "In some ways it was actually worse, but in some ways it was better."

"What do you mean?"

"Well, most of the kids hate me."

"Oh, Sally . . ." Emily protested.

"It's true," said Sally. "Maybe no one ever hated me before, but they do now. Only it doesn't matter too much, because I do have two friends, two kids who came today."

"Mom'll be glad to hear that," Emily said. "Who are they?"

"One is Melanie and one is Marty. They live in New Hebron, on the same street, and they've known each other a long time."

"Is Marty cute?"

"Oh, yes," Sally said. "He's really cute. He likes Melanie. But I don't think she likes him. I mean, she likes him as a friend, that's all. How's Petey doing with Coopy?"

"Ask her," Emily suggested.

Sally did, and then had to spend most of the trip

home listening to an incredibly boring recital of every single move Coopy Palmer had made all day.

"I guess you didn't take your eyes off him for one second," Sally said at last.

"Well," Petey sniffed, "if you didn't want to know, why did you ask me?"

Another time, Sally might have said something to placate Petey. Today she kept her mouth shut.

"Have you forgiven me?" Emily asked. "I mean for this morning—for my not thinking it was such a bad idea we were separated."

Sally shrugged.

"I guess you haven't," said Emily. "Well, I don't care. Really, I don't." She turned toward Petey. "Francine Hughes likes Coopy, too, but he told Dick Dresowitz he just barfs at the sight of her. I think you have a good chance, Petey."

More drivel about Coopy Palmer. Sally turned off her ears and shut her eyes.

Mom seemed pretty good that evening. They went out for dinner. Mom ate half a plate of pasta and drank almost a whole glass of wine. "When you kids go back to school," she said, "I'm going back to work."

"Don't you think you ought to wait until you're done with chemo?" Lisa suggested.

The further away Mom was from a chemo treatment, the better she felt, physically and mentally. Her best days were halfway in between two treatments. "No," she replied. "I'd be better off working. It's not good to sit home and think about things. I'd go back now, but it's August. I never worked in August, anyway."

"No, you didn't," said Sally. "Because we always went to the beach in August."

Mom let the crack pass. "It's slow in August. Wilbur can manage perfectly well without me." Wilbur was her partner in the travel agency. "Otherwise I'd go back now."

But the next day, when Emily and Sally got off the van and came into the house, it was their grandmother, not their mother, who was waiting for them in the kitchen. They both knew immediately that something was wrong. "Where's Mom?" Emily asked.

"She's in the hospital," Grandma said. "But don't worry, it's not serious."

Don't worry. That's what everyone always said, don't worry. Sally thought it was the most ridiculous phrase in the English language. Their mother was in the hospital, and they weren't supposed to worry? What did people think they were, dumb? Sally had expected more sense from her grandmother.

"What happened?" Emily asked.

"This morning she spiked a fever."

"That doesn't sound so bad," said Emily.

"It isn't," her grandmother assured her. "But you know, when you're on chemotherapy, they're very cautious. Those drugs they're giving her make it hard for her body to fight off infections. So when another person might just have a little cold, your mother runs a fever, and they have to put her in the hospital so they can shoot a whole lot of antibiotics directly into her veins. She'll be home tomorrow, Friday at the latest."

"Where's Dad?" Sally wanted to know.

"With her. He'll be home for dinner. I'll make hamburgers and French fries, and Lisa can cut up a nice salad. Gramps'll come over and eat here with us. That'll be fun, won't it?"

"Oh, sure," Sally said. "A blast."

"Listen, Sally," her grandmother insisted, "you don't have to worry. Your mother will be fine. After dinner, you and Emily and Lisa can go to the hospital with your dad and visit her."

Involuntarily, Sally's hand went to her breast. She remembered visiting her mother after surgery in May. Through the half-open hospital gown, Sally had glimpsed the bandages that covered the place where her mother's left breast had been. Some kind of clear liquid dripped from a bottle suspended on a metal rack, through a rubber tube, then out through a needle stuck into her arm. She was as pale as the pillowcase under her head, her dark hair clinging dank and lifeless to her cheeks. Her eyes were shut when they first stood by her bed, and for a fleeting second Sally was sure she was dead. Then Mom realized they were there, opened her eyes, and spoke to them. They had to lean over to catch her whispered words. Dad said she hadn't yet totally recovered from the anesthetic.

When they came back the next day, she was still pale, but she was sitting up. Her hair was combed, and she was wearing lipstick and one of her own pretty nightgowns. The television was blaring, and she waved her hands around as she spoke, just like her regular self.

But Sally had not forgotten that moment when she had looked at her mother and thought she was dead. She didn't want to go to the hospital after dinner. But she couldn't tell that to anyone. There was no way to tell *anything* to anyone. Once she got there, however, she had to admit to herself that her mother did look all right. Her cheeks were flushed and her eyes bright. Maybe that was because of the fever. Whatever the reason, it was better than seeing her white and silent.

"I don't think I'll go to camp tomorrow," Sally said in the car on the way home. "I'll stay home and get things ready in case they let Mom out."

"What's there to get ready?" Lisa asked. "If anything has to be done, Grandma will do it. The best thing you can do for Mom is to go about your life exactly as usual. She doesn't need to worry about where you are and what you're doing, on top of everything else."

"Oh, Lisa, just shut up," Sally snapped.

"Girls, girls," Dad interjected automatically, "stop fighting."

"I'm not fighting," Lisa said. "She's fighting."

"If I were going about my life exactly as usual," Sally complained, "I'd be at the beach."

"On the one hand, you want to stay home and help your mother. On the other hand, you want to be two hours away, at the beach. Which is it, Sally?" Dad's voice cut her like a knife. She sank back into the corner of her seat and didn't say another word the rest of the way home.

In the living room, she took the Shakespeare book off the shelf and found *Twelfth Night.*

> Act I, Scene I
> *Enter Orsino, Duke of Illyria, Curio, and*
>   *other lords; musicians attending*
> *Duke.* If music be the food of love, play
>   on,
> Give me excess of it; that surfeiting,
> The appetite may sicken, and so die.
> That strain again, it had a dying fall;
> O, it came o'er my ear like the sweet
>   sound

That breathes upon a bank of violets,
Stealing and giving odor.

Sally was a good reader, but the language of the play was too difficult even for her. She knew most of the words; "surfeiting" was really the only one she'd never seen before. But they were put together in ways that made it hard for her to figure out the meaning of the sentences. Even though the language was English, it was an English from which she was separated by four hundred years and the whole Atlantic Ocean. She didn't have the patience to struggle with it.

But in front of the play was a summary of the plot in modern prose. This she read. It wasn't nearly as lively or as detailed as Claire's version, but it fixed the story in her mind.

When she went to bed, the picture of her mother lying in the hospital right after surgery stood between her and sleep. She shut her eyes and inside her head started telling herself Viola's story. It worked. Before she was even a quarter of the way through, she drifted off to sleep.

T H R E E

Cliff Breakwater taught the Apaches canoeing. Camp Totem owned only three canoes. The small man-made lake, half taken up with swimming cribs, could accommodate no more at one time. Five Apaches plus Cliff were out on the lake, two in each canoe, while the rest waited their turns on the shore with Gerald.

"I'll go out with you, Melanie," Marty said.

"No," said Melanie. "I'm going with Sally."

"Who will Marty go with?" Sally asked.

Melanie dismissed the question with a wave of her hand. "He can ask one of the other kids."

"I'm not exactly Mr. Popularity around here," Marty said.

"Neither am I," said Sally. "Neither is Melanie.

Too bad we're not Senecas. The Senecas are much nicer."

"How do you know?" Melanie asked.

"My sister told me—my twin sister. She's a Seneca, and so are our friends, Petey and Gloria."

"What's it like to be a twin?" Melanie asked.

"I don't even know anymore," Sally replied. "It seems to me I hardly ever see her."

"Well, if you two are going out together, I'd better find someone," Marty said.

"You can ask Gerald to fix you up," Melanie suggested.

"That's probably the worst thing I could do," Marty retorted.

Sally watched him as he wandered off to join Maxie and Gil. They were dropping stones into the lake, staring as the circles they made spread out in the water. Marty picked up some stones and started dropping them, too.

"Let's walk around the lake," Melanie suggested. "It'll be a long time before our turn comes."

"No," said Sally. "I want to see how Marty makes out." Followed by Melanie, she strolled over to the trio at the water's edge. Fortunately, Angelo was out on the lake in Cliff's canoe.

"This is boring," Maxie was saying. "My father didn't dish out five hundred bucks for me to be bored."

"We're too old for this camp," Marty said. "They don't have the right things to do for people our age."

"Nothing we can do about it," Gil remarked.

"Yeah? Who says?" Marty picked up a stone, drew his arm back as far as it would go, and hurled the stone into the middle of the lake. "We ought to be able to think of something."

"At least you're a better stone thrower than you are a fire maker," Maxie replied. His round belly didn't affect his throwing arm. His stone went farther than Marty's. Gil, Sally, and Melanie threw stones, too, but none of theirs flew as far as the first two.

"You win, Maxie," Marty said. "Want to try for the best out of three?"

"Let it be between the two of you," Sally said. "None of the rest of us came even close."

Along the water's edge, Marty and Maxie began searching for the perfect stones. But a moment later, Gerald appeared. "Hey, you guys," he said, "no more throwing stones. You could hurt somebody. This is a small lake."

"We're dying of boredom," said Maxie. "What kind of camp is this, where people just stand around? I'm going to tell my father; he'll pull me out of here."

"Is that a threat," Gerald asked, "or a promise?"

"I could tell you a story," Sally offered. "You know, while we're waiting."

"What kind of story?" Maxie's eyes narrowed suspiciously.

"Just a story," Sally said. "About twins." She decided not to mention that it was a story from a play by Shakespeare.

"Who wants to hear a story?" Gil said. "Stories are for baby tribes like the Seminoles."

"You got something else to do?" Marty sat down. "Go ahead, Sally, tell."

And so she did. She wasn't a super storyteller, like Claire, but she was good enough. Marty, Melanie, Gil, and Maxie sat in a circle and absorbed every word that came out of her mouth. Maybe that was because she was right there in the circle with them, and they could see the expressions on her face and the gestures she made with her hands as she spoke. Or maybe it was because of Viola and Sebastian's story itself, so silly and so wonderful all at the same time.

Sally was only about halfway through when the canoes pulled into the dock. Gerald came back to tell them it was their turn.

"Maybe you can finish the story later," said Melanie.

Sally nodded.

"What story?" Gerald asked.

"Sally is telling us a good story," Melanie explained.

"A crazy story," said Maxie.

"But good," Melanie insisted.

"I feel as if I heard it somewhere before," Marty said. "But that doesn't matter. I want to hear the rest."

"Maybe you can tell it to the whole tribe," Gerald suggested.

Sally wasn't at all sure she wanted to tell the story to the whole tribe. It might not work so well with a big group. They might think the story was just plain silly, without the wonderful. Besides, she didn't feel like starting all over again. "Maybe I can tell the whole tribe a different story," Sally said. "From the beginning. If there's time. Which there probably won't be."

"Oh, we can make time," said Gerald.

They started toward the dock. Marty and Maxie headed for Angelo's canoe. "Hey, Maxie, don't go out with *him*," Angelo yelled, pointing an accusing finger at Marty. "You'll drown."

"Oh, don't worry about it," Maxie said. "He's okay."

"I'll talk to you later," Angelo warned.

They were out on the lake much longer than the others had been. Sally was glad they'd gone last, because they got to use up the rest of the day. When they finally returned to shore, it was time to go home.

In the dentist's waiting room, Sally thumbed through a copy of *People* magazine. Grandma had dropped her at the office, then driven off to the supermarket with

Emily. Grandma was stocking up because the next day Mother was to come home. "I'll buy artichokes and brie cheese and chocolate truffles and all the things your mother loves," she said.

"Don't bother," Sally replied. "She hasn't eaten any of that stuff since she's been on chemo. She has no appetite. She's tried three different medicines for nausea, and not one of them has worked."

"If the goodies are in the house, maybe she'll be tempted." Grandma was like Emily. She never seemed discouraged.

Sally glanced at a headline in the magazine. "Anne Milliken Battles Cancer." With a furious gesture, she threw the magazine onto the table. Then she picked it up again and started to read the article.

Sally had never heard of Anne Milliken. She turned out to be the star of a popular soap opera. She'd had *both* breasts removed. Her mother and her aunt had *died* of breast cancer. She was *still* taking chemotherapy. But she wasn't letting it get her down. Oh, no, not Anne Milliken. She went to work every day. When she came home, she gave the nanny the evening off, fed her two little girls their supper, and put them to bed herself. In her spare time, she did volunteer work for the American Cancer Society. "It's important for someone like me to serve as a role model," Anne Milliken said. "You can't give in to cancer. After all, it's only a disease."

Luckily, the receptionist called Sally into the examining room before she read any more. Otherwise she might have vomited, as if she were the one on chemotherapy. Why had she read that stupid article? She ought to know better by now, but every time she picked up a magazine with an article about cancer in it, she read it. She told herself she wasn't going to, but then she always did. They were all disgusting— the depressing ones, the hopeful ones, it didn't make any difference. Still she read them. She wondered if Emily read them. One day maybe she would ask her.

Dr. Gold examined her teeth after Phyllis, the hygienist, had cleaned them. Dr. Gold came back into the room to report on the X rays he'd taken. "Perfect," he said. "You don't have to come back for six months." He peered into her face. "What's the matter with you, Sally? I just gave you good news. 'Look, Ma, no cavities!' Can't you crack just the teeniest smile?"

"Yeah, Dr. Gold, thanks." She managed to curl her mouth upward into a semblance of a grin. Then she hopped out of the chair. In the outer office, she said to the nurse, "I'll wait for my ride outside. Just send the bill, like always."

She sat on the front steps. Of course she didn't have any cavities. She wouldn't have anything wrong with her as unimportant as a little hole in her tooth. Mom had perfect teeth, too. Sally figured that when something happened to her, it would be something that could really do a person in, like cancer. She'd never in her life had even a headache. A stomach-ache or the flu maybe, once every other year or so. Her body was saving up for the big whammy. She was sure of it.

When they got home, Grandma suggested the twins help her make a lemon meringue pie, another of Mom's favorites. "Count me out," Sally said. "It's too hot to bake." She went upstairs, locked herself in the bath-room, took off her clothes, and examined her naked body minutely. Except for a couple of mosquito bites, there wasn't a lump anyplace. But that didn't mean anything. When Mother was eleven, she probably didn't have any lumps on her, either.

"We'll have some time after lunch," Gerald told Sally the next morning as she arrived at the Apache tent, alone as usual. Once again Claire had gotten lost; once again the van had been late. "Maybe you can tell us a story then."

"Oh, not today, Gerald," she said. "I don't feel like it today." And she didn't. She was wondering about what she would find when she went home that afternoon. How would her mother look? How would her mother be? She didn't have any other stories in her head. "First let me finish the one I was telling Melanie and those guys yesterday," she added.

"You could start it over again, from the beginning, and tell it to everyone."

"No," she replied firmly. "I don't want to do that. It would be too boring for the kids who'd heard the first half." That probably wasn't true. She and Emily read books or watched videos they liked over and over again. She supposed other kids did, too. But it was a good excuse.

"Tomorrow maybe?" Gerald asked.

Sally shrugged. "Maybe." Actually, it was pretty neat to have the counselor so anxious for her to do something. But she wasn't going to give in today. Today she had other things on her mind. Besides, Gerald was a crummy counselor, spending every second he could with that Amy. He didn't deserve any help.

She hung around with Melanie and Marty. When they said something to her, she answered, but her replies were automatic. She scarcely knew what she was saying. As the day passed, her worry about her mother's return home grew larger and larger until it took up her whole brain. There was no room for anything else.

On the way home, she felt as if her head would burst. Claire, of course, got lost again. Sally didn't know whether that was a good thing or a bad thing. On the one hand, she was anxious to get home and see for herself how her mother was doing. On the other hand, if she wasn't doing well, maybe the longer it took to find that out the better.

"This is really a classic," Claire announced. "We're good and lost this time." She slowed the bus down and peered out at the street sign. "Conklin Street and Pascack Drive," she said. "Does anyone know where we are?"

Sally, Emily, Petey, and Gloria looked at each other. "I never heard of those streets," Petey said. "I bet we're not even in Watch Mountain."

"I bet we're not even in New Hebron," Gloria said.

"I bet we're not anywhere," Sally said.

"It could be hours before you guys get home," Claire said. "I guess I'd better tell you another story."

"Hey, Claire," Emily called out, "maybe instead of telling a story, it would be a good idea if you concentrated on the map."

"I can do two things at once. Even three," Claire replied, her voice bright with confidence. But she ran her hand through her hair again. It seemed to Sally that she always did that when she was nervous.

"Yeah, I bet," Emily muttered, settling back into her seat.

Sally listened to the story. The same thing happened this time that had happened last time. The story filled up her mind. While she was listening to it, there wasn't any room in her head for anything else.

F O U R

"Along, long time ago," Claire began, "on a stormy heath in Scotland, three witches danced around a boiling caldron."

The silence in the van was absolute. Everyone was interested in witches. But the story wasn't really about witches. It was about a man named Macbeth. The witches told him he'd be king of Scotland one day. He wanted to be king of Scotland. His wife, Lady Macbeth, wanted him to be king of Scotland even more than he wanted it. She egged him on until he murdered the king. He was crowned all right, but most Scots weren't happy about their new ruler. In order to protect his throne, he killed one person after another, until he was up to his neck in blood. But he and Lady Macbeth weren't happy. Besides the witches, ghosts and horrid visions haunted them, and at the end they got theirs.

Sally had never heard such a bloody story. It made an episode of "Miami Vice" seem as tame as "Sesame Street." For a moment after Claire stopped talking, no one in the van said a word. Then Emily asked, "Was that by Shakespeare, too?"

"Yes," Claire replied. "Its a play called—guess what?—*Macbeth.*"

"All that blood," Emily said, "and those witches. It would make a great horror movie."

"It ought to," Claire agreed. "People have tried— some really good people—but it's never quite worked out. I don't know why."

Wait till she told this one to the Apaches, Sally thought. It would blow their minds. Gerald might think it was too gory, but she didn't care about that. Sally knew she wouldn't be able to remember all the quotations Claire had used, but she thought the story would be good enough without them. She'd check it out in the Shakespeare book before she told it.

They were in Watch Mountain now. Somehow, while she was telling the story, Claire had found her way. One by one, she dropped off the other kids, arriving finally at Sally and Emily's house.

"It sounds like you know these plays by heart," Sally said. "All the lines and everything."

"Not all the lines," Claire replied. "Just some of them. And I'm not sure I got even those right."

"Were you an actress or something?" Emily asked.

"When I was younger, yes."

"And now you're a van driver." Sally regretted the words as soon as they were out of her mouth. "I'm sorry . . ." she murmured.

Claire laughed. "That's okay. I have to be something. Look at me. I could hardly be an actress anymore." Claire was so heavy that her hips dripped over the edges of the driver's seat, and the fat of her upper arms jiggled like jelly as she turned the wheel. Because of her pure white hair, Sally figured she must be at least as old as Grandma, though she was much taller, nearly six feet. Her face was still pretty, with smooth, fair skin, a rosebud mouth painted with pink lipstick, a small, turned-up nose, eyes as blue as a summer sky, and even at her age, a sprinkling of freckles across her pink cheeks.

Sally leaned her head over the back of Claire's seat. "I love being in plays. I'd like to be an actress when I grow up. Mom says I should be a lawyer. She says it's too hard to make a living as an actress."

"Tell me about it," Claire murmured.

"Would we have heard of you?" Emily asked. "I mean when you were an actress."

Claire laughed again. "No," she said. "I played bit parts in the movies, mostly. In one picture I had some lines. It was called *The Rose of Tralee*. Did you ever hear of it?"

Sally and Emily both shook their heads.

"I didn't think so," said Claire. "It never even shows up on late-night TV. I studied acting a lot, at schools and with private teachers. So that's why I know so much Shakespeare. I love him."

"If you worked in Hollywood," Sally asked, "how did you ever end up in Watch Mountain, New Jersey?"

"I don't live in Watch Mountain," Claire said. "I live over in Lenape with my daughter. I hadn't gotten any work out West for a long time, so when she got sick, I came here to help her. She's divorced, with two kids. Thank God, she's okay now."

"What'd she have?" Sally asked.

"Cancer," said Claire. "Colon cancer."

"And she's okay now?"

"Yes. They got it all out."

"How can you be sure?"

Claire pulled her hand through her hair. "Well, I can't be, I guess. But there's no reason to believe otherwise. Anyway, nothing in this life is *sure*." For a moment, she stared intently at Sally. "What's the matter, Sally? What are you so worried about?"

"My mother has cancer," Sally said. "They chopped off her breast. Now she takes chemotherapy and it makes her sick."

Claire nodded. "I know. It made Bev sick, too. Bev is my daughter. It's poison, but it works. It wouldn't kill the cancer cells if it weren't poison. And once you're done with it, you go back to feeling like your normal self."

"I never knew a Hollywood star before," Emily said.

Sally stood up. "We'd better go in now. Mom came home from the hospital this afternoon. We have to see how she is."

"Well, sure you do," Claire said. "Go ahead with you now. Maybe another day, I could come in and meet your mother."

"Yeah," Sally said. "Maybe you could tell her a story. I bet she'd like that."

Sally found Grandma in the kitchen setting a pot of tea, a cup, and a slice of lemon meringue pie on a tray. "Where's Mom?" she asked.

"In bed," Grandma replied.

"I thought she was okay. Why did they let her out of the hospital if she's not okay?"

"She is okay," Grandma said. "Just a little tired, that's all. Your dad picked her up; then he went back to work. Now that you kids are home, I think I'll leave, too. Your dad's bringing Kentucky Fried home for supper. Isn't that a treat!"

"Is it?" Sally retorted.

"Your mom thinks so." Grandma placed a paper

napkin on the tray. "Carry this up, please, Sally. Tell her I've gone, and I'll phone her later."

Sally longed to clutch at the hem of Grandma's skirt and cry "Don't go. Please don't leave me." But she wasn't three; she couldn't do that.

Just then Emily came in. "What were you doing out there?" Sally asked.

"Oh, talking some more to Claire."

For some reason, that annoyed Sally. "You should have come in. Grandma has to go home. We have to help."

But Emily wasn't listening. She'd run out of the room and up the stairs before Sally had finished her sentence.

Sally lifted the tray from the table and carried it upstairs, moving very slowly so the tea wouldn't slosh. The pot was covered. Unless a pot's been overfilled, tea is not likely to slosh out of a spout. She went slowly, anyway.

Mom was sitting up in bed. Emily was sitting next to her, chattering like a bird. "Well, all right, I'll tell you. I'm not supposed to, but I will. We decided to put up a tepee for the powwow. We're going to make it ourselves. I think we'll win, don't you? No one's ever made a whole tepee before."

"I'm sure you'll win," Mom said, smiling. Then she noticed Sally coming through the door. "Unless Sally's tribe wins, of course. Couldn't there be a tie?"

"We won't win." Sally said. "We haven't even decided what to do."

"There's still three weeks to go," said Mom. "You have time."

Sally set the tray on her mother's knees. "Oh, Sally thank you," Mom said.

"Don't thank me," said Sally. "Grandma made it. She said to tell you she went home. She'll call later." For a moment Sally hesitated. Then she asked the inevitable question. "How're you feeling, Mom?"

"Fine."

"If you're feeling fine, then why are you in bed?"

"I'm just a little tired, that's all. I'll be down for supper."

"Kentucky Fried," Emily said. "Mmmmmmm."

Sally glared at her sister. Whenever they had Kentucky Fried, Emily never touched the chicken or the cole slaw. All she ate were the French fries. She was just being jolly for Mother. It made Sally want to hit her. "I guess I'll take a shower," she said. "I'm hot."

"Don't you want to tell me about your day?" Mother asked.

"Like I said, the Apaches don't do anything. They're very boring." Sally picked up the remote from the top of the TV and handed it to her mother. "You can watch TV," she suggested.

Mother laid the remote on her bed table. "Nothing on in the afternoon."

"Do you want me to get you a book? A magazine? Maybe *Newsweek* came today. I could check."

"No," Mother returned sharply. "I don't want to read. I want to talk to you and Emily."

Wearily, Sally collapsed on the floor next to the bed. Immediately, Emily picked up where she'd left off. "Petey is still trying to be Coopy Palmer's girlfriend. But I told her, Coopy isn't interested in girls yet. Lots of boys are very slow that way."

Mom laughed. "Yeah, but they catch up eventually. Tell Petey to be patient."

"Petey doesn't know about patience," Sally said.

"Aha, a voice from the depths." Mom leaned over the edge of the bed. "Any nice boys in your tribe, Sally?"

"I told you. The Apaches are boring. All of them." Marty was a nice boy. Sally knew he was a nice boy. She just didn't feel like going into it.

"You're pretty boring yourself, Sally," Mother said. "What's the matter with you?"

A scream rose in Sally's throat. *You want to know what's the matter with me, Mom? You're sick. Maybe you're going to die. Maybe I'm going to die. That's what's the matter with me.* But she swallowed the words, she swallowed the scream. At the back of her tongue, it seemed as if she could taste her own blood. Then she had an idea. "I could tell you a story," she said.

Mom's eyebrows rose in surprise. "That might be nice," she said. "What story?"

"It's a very bloody story, but it's good. Maybe you know it." After all, the Shakespeare book was Mom's. "It's called *Macbeth.*"

"Oh, I read it a long time ago," Mom said. "I've forgotten the details. I don't mind hearing it again. In fact, I'd like to."

"Well," Emily said, "then *I'll* go take a shower, because I just heard it."

"From whom?" Mother asked.

"Remember the lady who drives the van? I told you about her."

"The one who's always getting lost," Mother said.

Sally nodded. "When she gets lost, she tells us stories. So I will tell one of those stories to you." It was good practice for Monday, when she might want to tell it to the Apaches.

Sally and Emily and their cousins Jenny and Jake had had a club called the Four Seasons since they were little. Grandma's sister, Aunt Nan, had directed them in plays they'd made up to present at family parties. Sally had been in plays at school, too. Telling a story was a little like being in a play. Better in a way—you got to perform all the parts.

Sally smiled. She was getting a lot of mileage out of Claire's stories. She hoped Claire would go on telling them. Did that mean she hoped Claire would go on getting lost? Well, if that was the price of the stories, maybe she did!

When Sally had finished telling Macbeth's story, Mother sighed. "And we think we've got troubles."

"Did I get it right?"

"Oh, I think so," Mother said. "How about finding the Shakespeare book for me? I'll check it out. You've made me want to read it again. You told it very well, Sally. I haven't seen so much life in you since the day Dad and I told you you couldn't go to the shore this summer."

Mother was pretty lively herself, all of a sudden. Sally ran down to the living room and picked up the enormous, illustrated volume. She carried it back upstairs, where her mother pored over it until Dad came home, clutching greasy paper boxes filled with fried chicken.

On Monday, Mom got up, made their breakfast, and packed their lunches. She seemed to be feeling pretty good, though Sally wondered what would happen when she went for her next chemotherapy treatment.

Once again, Claire got lost on her way to camp. The kids in the van couldn't help her, because she never got lost on the same streets twice. She managed to discover neighborhoods in central New Jersey that none of the campers had even imagined were there.

Sally was sitting next to her. "Tell us another story," she asked.

"I only tell stories coming home," Claire replied. "I never tell stories going. Going I have to concentrate."

"Friday you said you could do two things at once."

"That all depends on which direction I'm traveling."

"Claire . . ."

"Yes?"

"I'm going to ask you a personal question." Sally felt she knew Claire well enough now. "You don't have to answer if you don't want to."

"That's right, I don't."

"You won't get mad, will you?"

"I don't know."

"I'll ask, anyway."

"Good."

"If you have such a lousy sense of direction, why did you take a job as a van driver?"

"You think anyone was going to hire a three-hundred-pound female giant to be a waitress or salesclerk? I don't have the skills to work in an office. But I'm a good driver. I've never had an accident. I've never even had a ticket. I passed the bus driver's test without any trouble."

"Because it didn't include a section on finding your way."

"I think that's enough from you, missy," Claire snapped.

"I knew you'd get mad," Sally said. "But don't, because I'm not sorry anymore that you get lost. If you didn't, there'd be no stories."

"That's better," Claire returned, mollified. "You sure do say what's on your mind."

"Only if it's not important," Sally murmured. Claire was busy glancing from the road to the map and back to the road again. Sally didn't know whether she'd heard her or not.

At camp, the Apaches were getting ready to follow a trail Cliff Breakwater had laid down through the woods. Cliff wouldn't be with them; they'd have to do it on their own, to see if they'd learned to read the Indian signs he'd taught them.

"Don't we need a chief?" Angelo asked. "Last session we had a chief. You know, someone to lead the way and to make decisions when we can't agree. And not just for this activity. We need a chief for lots of things, especially the powwow."

"Isn't that Gerald?" Melanie asked.

"It's definitely not me." Gerald wasn't interested in any more responsibility than he already had. "It has to be a camper, doesn't it, Angelo?"

"Yeah," Angelo agreed. "But you've got to pick him. Or her. That's what Arnie did last session." Sally wondered what had happened to Arnie. Oh, well;

Amy was awfully cute. If Arnie had still been the Apache counselor, he'd probably have fallen for her, too.

"We're not babies," Maxie said. "We can choose our own chief." He leaned back against a tree and smiled. He was happy, Sally thought, because something might happen at last.

"How do you choose a chief?" Melanie asked.

"Same way you choose anyone, I guess, " said Gerald. "You elect him—or her."

"I nominate Marty," Sally said.

"I nominate Sally," Melanie said.

Sally's response was unhesitating. "I decline."

Lightly, Angelo punched Gil's arm. Gil turned and stared at him. Angelo frowned and punched him again. At last Gil understood. "I nominate Angelo," he said.

"Sally, you can't decline," said Melanie.

"I nominated Marty." Sally enunciated each word carefully, as if Melanie were hard of hearing. "If I want Marty, why would I run against him?"

"I don't think Indians elected their chiefs," Angelo said. "I think they were chosen for their powers—the strongest, the fastest, the best hunter, something like that. We'll have to have a contest. Some kind of race maybe." Angelo was very fast.

"I'm sure some Indians elected their chiefs," Sally insisted.

"Well, we could have a contest, if you'd rather," Gerald said.

"We could throw stones in the lake," Maxie suggested. "Or a ball at a target."

"Listen, Maxie," Angelo snapped, "no one nominated you."

"I nominate Maxie," Gil said.

"It's either a contest or an election," said Sally. "It can't be both."

"I nominate Maxie, anyway," Gil said.

"You can't do that, dummy," Angelo said. "You've already nominated me."

"I've got an idea," said Gerald. "We'll have several contests. We'll have a race, we'll throw a ball at a target. . . ."

"We'll tell stories," Marty suggested.

"That's not fair, " Angelo said. "Sally's the only one who tells stories."

"Is a race fair?" Marty asked. "Everyone knows you'll win."

"Read my lips," Sally said. "I don't want to be chief. This is between Angelo and Marty." And Marty had better win, she thought. If he didn't, she'd leave this camp at last—that was for sure.

"What about Maxie?" Gil asked. Angelo punched him once again, this time hard.

"It's between Angelo and Marty," Maxie said.

"Everyone has to participate," Gerald announced. "This is not a camp for watchers. This is a camp for doers."

"Did my father call you?" Maxie asked.

Gerald glared at him. "I didn't need a phone call from your father. I know how this place is supposed to be run. The canoeing—that was just one thing. It couldn't be helped." Gerald struck his head with the flat of his hand. "But what am I explaining myself to a kid for? I must be going crazy."

Gerald, usually dreaming droopily of Amy, was suddenly as full of energy as an electric wire. He jumped to his feet to organize the race, which, as they'd all expected, Angelo won easily.

"One point for Angelo," Marty said. "No points for me."

"How many points does it take to be chief?" Gil asked.

"I don't know," Gerald said.

"How about twenty-one?" Maxie suggested. "Twenty-one is a good number."

"Any objections?" Gerald looked first at Marty and then at Angelo. Neither of them said a word. Gerald rubbed his hands together. For the first time in days, he looked really happy. Between Sally's stories and twenty-one contests, he would no longer have to struggle thinking up activities to fill empty spaces in the program, which really was geared to the younger campers. The kids had saved him.

"Two points for the one who finds the most clues on the trail," Gerald said.

Angelo was not very good at picking up the tiny clues Cliff Breakwater had left in the woods. But sharp-eyed Marty quickly noticed the little pile of stones, the scratch on the birch tree, the pointed pine cones. If it hadn't been for him, they'd never have found the watermelon hidden in a hole in the ground at the end of the trail.

"Now the score is two to one," Sally announced, as they returned to their tent to eat their prize.

"If the trail was worth two points," Angelo said, "then fire making has got to be worth at least two points, too. I won the fire making, so the score is really three to two."

"But that wasn't a contest," Sally cried.

"Everything's a contest," Angelo said.

"It's not fair to make it a contest afterward," Sally insisted.

Angelo glared at her. "Could you have done any better if you'd known? We'll take a vote. Was the fire making a contest or not?"

The vote was eight to two against Angelo. The only one who voted with Angelo was Gil, probably because Angelo had forced his arm up when Gerald called "All in favor?" Sally knew that because she peeked through her fingers, even though in the interest of a secret ballot, they were supposed to shut their eyes and cover them with their hands.

"I have an idea," Marty said. "For the powwow."

"We don't want to hear it," said Angelo. "You're not chief yet. And I don't think you ever will be."

"Do we have to wait until we have a chief to talk about the powwow?" Marty inquired.

"I thought you thought the powwow was silly," Gil remarked.

"It doesn't have to be," Marty replied. "It all depends on what we do for it."

Melanie turned to Gerald. "Does everything at the powwow have to be one hundred percent Indian?"

Gerald rubbed his chin. "No one ever said it did. No one ever said it didn't."

"Then I guess we can do what we want," Marty said. "It doesn't matter if we win or not. What matters is having fun."

Angelo jumped to his feet. "You're a fathead, Marty. You're the biggest nerd in the state of New Jersey. If we listen to you, this tribe will end up at the bottom of the pile. We'll be nothing but a bad joke around here." He placed his hands on his hips, put on a falsetto voice, and jerked his head from side to side as he quoted Marty. " 'It doesn't matter if we win or not. What matters is having fun.' You sound like a total wimp. You *are* a total wimp."

"All right, smarty-pants," Sally said. "Before you call people names because you don't like their ideas, which you haven't even heard, how about telling us what *you* think we ought to do for the powwow?"

Gerald waved his hands helplessly. "Kids, please, no fighting."

Angelo ignored him. "Don't you see, jerko?" he told Marty. "That's the prize. The person who gets to be chief gets to choose what we do at the powwow. So I'm not telling you my idea until I'm chief. You keep your mouth shut, too, Marty."

"Well, okay," Marty agreed.

"Because if you don't, I'll knock your block off."

Being chief was so important to Angelo, Sally thought, that knocking Marty's block off was something he might actually do. He wasn't going to be chief, though. Not if Sally could help it.

F   I   V   E

Petey and Gloria didn't ride the van home. Their mothers picked them up from camp to take them shopping and out for supper. Sally watched them drive off in Petey's mother's little station wagon, envy squeezing her heart. She had loved it when her mother had taken her shopping and for supper in the mall. Mom used to take them in turn. She said it was a way to have special alone time with each one of her kids. But none of them—not Lisa or Sally or Emily—had gone out alone with Mom for months and months and months. Sally wondered if it would ever happen again.

"So what are the Apaches going to do for the powwow?" Emily asked when she and Sally were seated next to each other in the van.

Emily was merely trying to make conversation. "It's a secret," Sally replied.

Emily's jaw dropped. "A secret from *me?*"

"From everybody," Sally said.

"But I told you what the Senecas are doing. I'm your twin. We don't have secrets."

"We're separated now," Sally retorted. "We're in different tribes. So now we do have secrets."

Emily sighed. "You're still mad at me."

"I'm not mad at you. There's nothing to be mad about."

"Then tell me."

"No."

"I bet you don't even know what you're going to do yet."

Sally made no reply. She shut her eyes and pretended to go to sleep. It was a trick she'd learned long ago for avoiding unwanted conversations. She didn't suppose that Emily really believed she was asleep, but it didn't matter. Emily said nothing, either. She was as silent as Sally herself.

The voices of the other kids rose and fell. Sometimes Claire spoke up and told them to shush. But Sally didn't open her eyes. She felt as if all the people on the bus were very, very far away, even Emily. She felt as if they were so far away they didn't even really exist. She felt as if she were absolutely alone, the only person on the entire planet. There was no one to talk to. Her feelings were like genies in stoppered bottles, locked up forever.

But when Claire started another story, she listened. This one was about another wicked king, Richard III of England. Like Macbeth, he murdered everyone in sight in order to get and hold on to his throne. He locked up his own little nephews in the Tower of London, then decided that wasn't sufficient and had them smothered.

Richard was a bitter, ugly man with a hump on his back, but still he had charm. He managed to seduce Lady Anne, the widow of the legitimate heir to the throne, even though she knew he was responsible for her husband's death. He actually talked her into marrying him.

At Bosworth Field, on the night before his last battle, he dreamed of eleven ghosts, the ghosts of all the people he had killed. The next day during the battle, he lost his mount and ran around the field crying, "A horse, a horse! my kingdom for a horse!" He didn't get a horse, and he didn't get to keep his kingdom, either. He was killed by the earl of Richmond, who was then crowned King Henry VII.

The story was supposed to be true, based on actual fact, though Claire said there were some historians who claimed that Richard III was nowhere near as black hearted as Shakespeare had painted him.

"Listen, Claire," Sally said as she was about to leave the van, "enough already with these murderous kings."

"Justice always triumphs at the end," Claire replied. "Anyway, I thought you guys liked gory stories."

"Well, we do," Sally admitted. The story had absorbed her, enthralled her, released her. "But we like silly stories, too, you know, like *Twelfth Night.*"

"Okay," said Claire. "Next time I'll tell you another silly one."

But there was no next time. Despite her claim that she could do two things at once, Claire spent the rest of the week concentrating on maps and street signs. Monday morning when Sally and Emily boarded the van, it was driven by a long-haired young man wearing a dirty undershirt and a purple visor.

"Who are you?" Emily asked immediately.

"Darley," he replied shortly. He didn't ask her who she was.

"Where's Claire?" Sally wondered.

"I don't know no Claire," he said.

"She drives this van."

"I drive this van."

"So what happened to Claire?"

Darley shrugged and stuck Walkman earphones in his ears. He didn't say another word the entire trip, which was very short, anyway. He picked up everyone on the route and deposited them at camp inside half an hour.

Sally decided she wasn't really surprised by Claire's disappearance. The whole weekend had been so awful that one more lousy thing was only to be expected. When she and Emily had walked into the house on Friday afternoon, Mom wasn't in the living room or in the kitchen. Grandma had driven her to the doctor for her chemotherapy that morning. They'd stuck the poison into her veins, and it had knocked her out as usual. As soon as she'd gotten home, she'd gone to bed. When Emily and Sally went up to see her, she kissed them and asked how their day went, but she didn't look or sound as if she really wanted to know. So Sally and Emily both said, "Fine," and left her to sleep, which was all she ever wanted to do after her chemotherapy treatments.

Emily went into their bedroom and turned on the TV, switching to a channel that showed cartoons in the late afternoon, followed by sitcom reruns.

"Let's switch channels and watch Judge Wapner," Sally suggested.

"I don't like Judge Wapner," Emily said.

She'd never said that before. It used to be they always watched TV together in their room. It used to be they reached some kind of compromise if they didn't agree on what to watch, like Sally could choose the first half hour, and Emily could choose the second, because it really was Sally's TV. She'd gotten it for Hanukkah in fourth grade, when Emily had wanted a ten-speed bike.

"It's my TV," Sally said. That was something she'd never said before.

Emily stood up and snapped off the set. "I'll watch in the family room," she announced, and marched downstairs.

Sally turned on "The People's Court." For some reason, today it wasn't very interesting. She flipped the channels and couldn't find anything she wanted to see, but she waited until the half hour was over before she went downstairs herself and out to the back porch to read.

She'd scarcely finished a chapter when Lisa arrived home from baby-sitting the Gregory kids. "You're early," Sally said.

"Yeah. Sometimes they get home early on Fridays. I'll start dinner. Come on inside and help me."

Sally fixed her eyes on her book.

"Come in and help me," Lisa repeated.

Still Sally made no reply.

Lisa walked over and tugged on a lock of Sally's hair. "I said, help me!"

"No." Sally stiffened. "I won't."

"What do you mean, you won't?"

"You're not my mother. You can't tell me what to do."

"But today's Mom's chemo day. She's probably fast asleep."

"That's what I mean. Just because she's sick doesn't make you the boss."

"My God!" Lisa said. "You're unbelievable." She hurried inside the house, slamming the screen door behind her. "Emily," she shouted, "where are you, Emily?"

Through the open windows, Sally heard Emily's reply, and then heard the two of them clattering companionably around the kitchen getting supper. Sally kept her book open on her lap, but mostly she listened to what they were saying—nothing unusual, just a regular ordinary everyday conversation about which one of them should peel the potatoes and whether or not Lisa should invite Mike Featherman to Kelly Imfeld's swim party. Sally was furious. How could they? How could they just stand there and talk about regular ordinary everyday stuff when Mom was lying there, right over their heads, feeling like she was going to die?

Mom didn't come down for diner. Lisa took her some roast chicken, mashed potatoes, and salad on a tray. When she came back she lit the Sabbath candles, covering her head with Mom's white lace scarf, placing her hands over her eyes, and chanting the Hebrew blessing with exactly the intonation Mom always used. It was not the first time she had done this since Mom had gotten sick. But it was the first time Sally had said anything about it. "Mom's supposed to do that," she muttered.

Lisa turned in surprise. "Mom isn't coming down to dinner. She asked me to do it."

"I don't think it counts if you do it."

"Of course it counts," said Dad. "If I were sick and you or Emily or Lisa sang the blessing over the wine, don't you think God would hear it just the same?"

Sally didn't think God had heard a single thing that was going on in the Berg house for months and months. But Dad sang the kiddush, the same way he always did. They all sat down, except Emily, who made the blessing over the bread.

"Sally and Emily, you serve the salad," Lisa said. "I'll get the next course."

Sally turned to her father. "Do you hear that, Dad?" she asked. "Who made her my boss?"

"She's the oldest," Dad said. "She's kind of taking charge. I have to work, and your grandmother has her own house and a husband and a job to worry about. I for one am very glad Lisa is doing what she does."

"Thank you, Dad," Lisa said.

She sounded so smug and self-satisfied, Sally felt

like pricking her with a needle. Maybe then she'd collapse, as if she were a balloon.

"She doesn't have to order me around," Sally complained. "I could take charge, or Emily."

"But you haven't, have you?" Dad said quietly.

"Emily helped me get dinner," Lisa said.

"Meaning I didn't?" Sally retorted.

"Well, did you?" Lisa asked.

"I would have if you'd asked me nicely."

Lisa plopped her elbows on the table and leaned her forehead into her palms. "My God," she said, "I don't have enough to do around here without treating my little sister as if she were some kind of princess."

"Girls, stop bickering," Dad said. "I really can't stand this kind of conversation at the dinner table."

"*I'm* not bickering," Emily said. Sally wanted to prick her, too.

"But, Dad," Lisa protested, "Sally is so . . ."

"You heard me, Lisa. Once again, thank you very much for all that you're doing. Emily, thank you, too. Sally, this is a difficult time for all of us. We're all on edge, and we must try to be patient with one another. Will you please help Emily serve the salad?"

Sally obeyed. The rest of the meal passed more or less in silence. They didn't sing Sabbath songs afterward. No one seemed to feel like it.

Saturday and Sunday were as bad as Friday night. Mom got dressed and came downstairs, which was good, but she didn't feel like going anyplace, and Dad didn't feel like going anywhere without her. Grandma and Grandpa were visiting Jenny and Jake at the shore for the weekend, so Sally and her family mostly just hung around the house, getting on one another's nerves. Actually, it was Sally who seemed to get on everyone else's nerves, and everyone else who seemed to get on Sally's nerves. She felt as if she were a stranger in her own home.

She had actually looked forward to returning to camp Monday morning. But instead of fat, funny Claire to talk with on the bus, there was only silent, sourpuss Darley. As soon as she got to the Apache tent, she asked Gerald if he knew what had happened to Claire.

"There were a lot of complaints about the kids not getting here on time," Gerald said. "I think the bus company fired her."

The very thing Sally herself had suggested at least twice at the beginning of camp. Only now, she felt sick about it.

The Apaches spent an hour in the arts and crafts tent learning from Cliff Breakwater how to stitch leather. Then they went swimming. Later, while they ate lunch, Sally told them the story of *Macbeth*. They liked Shakespeare's horror story as much as the van passengers had.

They were eating in a small grove of hemlock trees on the far side of the lake. Sally knew they were hemlock trees because Cliff Breakwater had told them. He'd made them learn the names of all the trees around camp. He said they were the kind of trees you saw every day everywhere in central New Jersey, and you ought to know their names, just the way you knew the names of the people who lived on your block.

Melanie had gathered a bunch of pine cones into a big pile. Angelo walked by and gave the pile a kick, scattering them all over the grove, erasing in an instant all of Melanie's effort. "Hey," she cried, "what do you think you're doing?"

"Isn't that what you made the pile for?" Angelo asked. "To kick?"

"I did not," she said. "I was going to take the cones to the crafts shop. We can make things out of them."

"Like what?" Angelo scoffed.

"Thanksgiving and Christmas decorations," Melanie said.

"Oh, who cares?" Angelo said.

"Me," Melanie insisted. "I care."

"We'll help you gather them up again," said Marty, rubbing his nose with his forefinger. Sally could never tell that Marty was upset from his tone of voice, but she'd learned that the finger on his nose was a dead giveaway. "Right, Gerald?" he added.

"Oh, yes," Gerald said.

"Angelo, too," said Sally.

Gerald glared at Angelo. "You, too, buddy."

With all the Apaches working, the pile was soon bigger than it had been before. Sally went by herself to the far corner of the grove and gathered pine cones into her khaki cap. It gave her a chance to think. "You know," she said as she returned to add her cache to the pile, "we have crafts at this camp, we have athletics, we have swimming, we have boating, we have nature, but there's one thing we don't have. We don't have any drama."

"We don't have anyone here qualified to do drama," Gerald said.

"Which is really too bad," Sally went on. "Because if we could do drama, we could put on a play for the powwow."

"A play?" Angelo scoffed. "A play? What's a play got to do with Indians? Anyway, Sally, what have you got to do with the powwow? The chief will decide."

Sally dismissed him with a wave of her hand. "Forget the powwow. I'm sorry I mentioned it. We should have drama, anyway. At our age, we need drama."

"Well . . ." Gerald hesitated. "I don't know. I could take it up with Ruth. But I told you. We don't have anyone here to do drama. I certainly can't."

"I know someone who could," Sally said. "But the camp would have to pay her something. She needs the money. Do you think you could ask Ruth about that?"

"Actually," Maxie said, "it says in the brochure that the camp has drama. But it doesn't. That's fraudulent advertising. Maybe I'll tell my father. My father's a lawyer. Actually, he's a very big lawyer. He does a lot of fraud cases."

"You don't need to threaten," Gerald said, and sighed. "I think you kids are getting a little out of hand."

"We're the oldest group," Marty said. "We have minds of our own."

"Yeah," Gerald agreed. "I should ask for a transfer to the Seminoles." He turned back to Sally. "I will ask Ruth about it. Who do you have in mind?"

Sally moved closer to Gerald. "Maybe I could just talk my idea over with you and Ruth first," she said softly.

Gerald shrugged. "I'll let you know."

"Who says we want to do plays?" said Angelo. "I hate plays."

"I hate arts and crafts," Sally said. "But I do them."

The important thing was getting Camp Totem to hire Claire, one way or another. "After all, it does say drama in the brochure." Her mother had given her a brochure, but she'd never actually read it. She'd been too angry at the whole idea of camp to do that. She was taking Maxie's word for it. She hoped he was right.

"What is it with you kids?" Gerald complained. "I never saw such a gang for reading the fine print. You all sound like lawyers."

Not all, Sally thought. Just me and Maxie. "But you will speak to Ruth?" she asked.

Gerald nodded. Then he dragged them all off to the athletic fields to play softball. The ten of them had to divide up into two teams. Sally wished they were playing against the Senecas. They never even got to see the Senecas. Marty and Angelo each had two hits, so the ball game did nothing to advance either one in the race for chiefdom. Sally was glad when the long, hot afternoon was over and she boarded the van for the trip home.

The van was yellow, and on its sides, in black letters, appeared the words CROSSLAND BUS COMPANY. When she got inside the house, Sally looked the name up in the phone book, found the number, and dialed it. "Crossland Bus Company," she heard a man's voice say.

"Are you Mr. Crossland?" Sally asked.

"No. That's just the name of the company. I'm Augie, the office manager."

"Hello, Augie. I'm looking for Claire."

"Claire doesn't work for us anymore," Augie replied.

"I know that. I was on her van. I'd like her name and phone number."

"I can't give out personal information."

"But I want to talk to her. She was so nice. I want to tell her that."

"It's not our policy . . ."

"Listen, Augie," Sally said, "I'm not a bill collector or a cop or anything like that. My name is Sally Berg, and I just turned eleven in July. Claire's my friend."

There was a long pause. Then, at last, Augie spoke again. "Claire *is* nice. She's a good driver, too. She just doesn't have any sense of direction. That's sort of missing in her brain. You know, like some people are color-blind."

"Yeah," Sally said, "I know. But no one's perfect."

The man laughed a little. "Well, that's true. However, not being able to find your way—that might not matter for an actor or a teacher. It's just kind of serious for a driver."

Funny that he said an actor or a teacher. Claire had already been an actor, and something like a teacher was what Sally had decided she ought to be.

"You sound like a good girl," Augie said. "So I'll tell you what I'm going to do. I'm going to take your phone number and give it to Claire. Then if she wants to, she can call you."

"Okay. It's seven two five, one four one five. And I'm Sally," she reminded him. "Sally Berg."

She hung up the phone, hoping that at this very moment Gerald was talking to Ruth as he'd promised. But she knew grown-ups. Sometimes they weren't very reliable. What was important to you didn't always seem important to them. Of course, Gerald wasn't exactly a grown-up. He was probably seventeen or eighteen. That made him a teenager—an old teenager, but still a teenager. Lisa was a teenager. And Lisa, though the most aggravating human being on the earth, was, Sally had to admit, thoroughly reliable. However, she had her doubts about Gerald.

S I X

Sally looked at the pictures in the Shakespeare book while she was waiting for Claire to call. She liked the picture from a play called *The Tempest* the best. It showed a man standing in front of a cave, wearing a magician's cape and carrying a wand, which he was pointing at a kind of monster, half man, half bear, who was cowering in front of him. She didn't read the plot summary. She wanted to hear the story from Claire.

But Claire never called. At ten Emily came upstairs. "Dad said to tell you it's time for bed." Mom had said good night soon after supper. "What've you been doing up here all by yourself all night?"

"Why shouldn't I stay up here by myself?" Sally

asked. "No one seems to enjoy my company these days."

"I'd put it the other way around," Emily retorted. "You don't enjoy our company."

Sally, already in her pajamas, climbed into bed and sat staring at the picture of the magician and the monster. Home was awful. It wasn't just that Mom was maybe dying, and Lisa was so bossy. The worst part was feeling as if she were separated from her twin by an ocean, like Viola and Sebastian in *Twelfth Night*. Camp wasn't much better. The Apaches had to take sides in the struggle between Marty and Angelo for chief. They were being torn apart. And that, Sally suddenly realized, was like *Macbeth* and *Richard the Third*. Now Claire had disappeared, and with her had gone her stories. There wasn't anything good in her life, not one single thing. If Sally were the crying type, she would have cried herself to sleep. Instead, she just stared at the picture until her eyes shut of their own accord and the book dropped out of her hand.

But the next morning, when she got to the Apache tent, Gerald took her aside and said, "Ruth wants to talk to you. Go on over during arts and crafts."

Sports came before arts and crafts. They went to the athletic fields for volleyball. Of course, Marty was captain of one team, Angelo of the other. "Five points," Angelo said. "Whichever team wins, it's five points toward being chief."

"What's the score now?" Melanie asked.

Gerald took a little piece of crumpled paper out of the pocket of his cutoffs. "We said the first guy to make twenty-one points would be chief. It's tied, fourteen to fourteen. Whoever wins the volleyball game will have a real leg up."

"Five points is too many," Maxie said.

Marty put his hand on Maxie's arm. "Five points is okay. Let's get this thing over with. I'm tired of it already."

"We get to choose our teams," Angelo said. "I choose Brian." Brian, at five feet four inches, was by far the tallest Apache, making him extremely desirable at the net.

"No," said Marty. "The teams get to choose us. Let the kids be on the team they want to be on."

"But then there won't be the same number of kids on each team," Gil pointed out. He looked worried. Sally figured he wanted to pick Marty's team, but was afraid Angelo would kill him if he did.

"Let Gerald pick the teams," Marty said. "That would be fairest."

"Hey, leave me out of this," Gerald said.

"You better," Melanie said. "Otherwise there'll be blood all over this field."

"Each captain could take turns picking a name from a hat," Gerald suggested hopefully.

"No good," said Maxie. "Then one team might end up with all the good players, and the other team with all the poor ones."

"Oh, all right," Gerald groaned. "I'll do it." It took him twenty minutes to pick the teams. It always took him a long time to make a decision, and he never made one unless some kid forced him to. Just about any one of the Apaches would have made a more effective counselor than he was. If the Apaches had a chief, maybe they'd no longer spend half the day arguing over every little thing. But then Angelo's team won the volleyball game, bringing Angelo within two points of victory. Angelo as the leader was worse than no leader at all, so far as Sally was concerned. She'd have to do something about it.

But at the moment, she didn't have the time. While the others made their way to the arts and crafts tent, she hurried down to the old farmhouse that served as Camp Totem's office. Ruth was waiting for her on the porch. They sat down on the wooden steps. "Well, Sally," Ruth said, "I hear you want some drama at Camp Totem."

"I like drama a lot more than arts and crafts or nature," Sally said. "The brochure said there'd be drama."

"We wanted to have drama," Ruth explained. "But the drama counselor we hired backed out at the last minute. She got an acting job at a summer theater out in Pennsylvania someplace. It was too late to replace her."

"I know someone who could be the drama counselor. She's not working right now."

"Who is she?" Ruth asked.

Sally hesitated. It didn't seem wise to utter Claire's name right off. "Well, it's someone who's not very good at some things. But she's very good at drama. She's had a lot of experience."

"That's not everything," Ruth said. "Is she good with kids?"

At least as good as Gerald, Sally felt like saying. But she didn't. She remembered the noisy van, hushed to silence by Claire's Shakespeare stories. "Yes," Sally replied firmly. "She's very good with kids."

"Tell me who she is, and I'll get in touch with her. We do have some money for a drama counselor. A little bit."

"It's Claire," Sally said. "She wouldn't be expensive."

"Claire?"

"Claire who drove the van."

"The one the bus company fired?"

"Well, like I said, there are some things she's not so good at."

"Why do you think she'd be good at being a drama counselor?"

Sally explained about Claire's parts in old movies and all the classes she'd taken and how much she knew about the theater. But mostly she talked about the Shakespeare stories Claire had told, and the way the whole van had listened to them as attentively as they did their favorite rock tapes.

"The least I can do after that testimonial is talk to her," Ruth said when Sally was done. "Give me her phone number."

"I don't know it."

"What's her last name?"

"I don't know that, either," Sally admitted.

Ruth uttered a dry little laugh. "Her number isn't going to be listed in the book under 'Claire.'"

"Yeah," Sally replied glumly, "I know. It probably won't be listed under her last name, either, whatever it is. She lives with her daughter, so it's probably listed under her daughter's name. I don't know that, either."

"I'd like to talk to Claire," Ruth said. "I really would. But how can I if I have no way to get in touch with her?"

Sally shook her head. "If I figure out a way, I'll let you know."

"Okay, Sally. You do that. Thanks for your concern. Camp Totem appreciates it."

"Yeah," Sally said again. Slowly she made her way down the dusty path, scuffing pebbles out of her way with the tips of her sneakers to help herself think. But she didn't come up with a single new idea. She'd gotten as far as she could with the bus company. The only thing left was to hope that Claire would call her. She'd better call soon. Otherwise it would be too late in the camp season to start a drama program.

When they got home that afternoon, Sally and Emily found their mother on the screened porch, sewing. Mom hated to sew. Dad and the girls had learned early to take care of their own missing buttons and split seams. For hems, they used to turn to Grandma, but now Lisa did them. Sally didn't know if needle and thread in Mom's hand was a good sign or a bad one.

Emily plopped down at the foot of the chaise. "What're you sewing?"

Mom shook out the scrunched-up garment in her hand. It was her red-and-white-striped bathing suit. "I'm putting in a pocket," she said, "for my prosthesis." That was the phony breast made out of spongy plastic Mom had bought to stick inside her bra where her real breast used to be.

Sally sat in the wicker rocking chair opposite the chaise and began to rock vigorously. "You haven't been swimming all summer," she said.

"I'll be swimming tomorrow," Mom replied with a

smile. "Ellen and Ralph Sloat invited me to spend a couple of days with them at the beach."

"You're going to the beach?" Sally exclaimed.

"Yes," Mom said. "Isn't that great? The Sloats' house is gorgeous. It was so nice of them to invite me."

"Who's going to take care of us?" Sally muttered.

"Dad'll be here, and Lisa. Grandma will look in. Anyway, you guys have gotten real independent. I'm proud of you."

"Will you see Jenny and Jake?" Sally asked.

"I'm sure I will," Mom said. "Maybe I'll have dinner there one night."

A picture of the cottage she knew so well filled Sally's mind. The grown-ups were sitting on the deck, sipping cocktails and chatting while they watched the daylight slowly die away over the ocean. Jenny and Jake were there, too, drinking sodas, eating corn chips, and noisily playing hand after hand of hearts. But instead of playing with Sally and Emily, the way they should have been, they were playing with other kids, kids Sally didn't even know.

"I don't think it's fair," she cried, the words jumping out of her mouth like bullets.

"What's not fair?" Mom asked.

"You get to go to the beach and we don't."

Mom was so startled that the bathing suit dropped out of her hand. Emily leaned over and picked it up. "I can't believe what I'm hearing," Mother said.

"We had to stay home because you're sick, but you

don't have to stay home because you're sick." Sally couldn't believe what she was hearing, either, even though it was coming out of her own mouth. It was if there were two Sallys, one who thought wicked thoughts and then said them out loud, and the old Sally, the Sally who used to be and way deep down still was. That Sally watched the horrid new Sally with as much surprise as her mother did.

"I'm not going away for two months," Mother said. "I'm going away for two days. Don't make a federal case out of it."

"Do you think you can drive that far?" Emily asked.

"Sure. It's only a couple of hours. It'll be twelve days since I've had a chemo treatment when I go, so I'll be at my best. I'll be just fine."

But Sally couldn't let the subject drop. "If you're so fine, then I really can't understand why you haven't taken us to the beach, at least for a weekend," she complained.

Her mother's eyes blazed. "I'm sick. I've got cancer. And you begrudge me two days at the beach? My God, Sally, what's the matter with you?"

"I don't know, Mom. I don't know what's the matter with me!"

Sally rushed off the porch, slamming the screen door behind her. She yanked her bike out of the garage, mounted it, and pedaled furiously down Bittersweet Drive and out onto Stony Hill Road.

"Come back. Sally, come back." She heard Emily's shouts pursuing her down the street, but she ignored them. In a few minutes, she reached the hill for which the road was named. Climbing it, she was forced to slow down. She didn't have a ten-speed bike, like Emily. Hers was just a rusty old relic that once had belonged to Lisa. By the time she got to the top of the hill, Emily, on Superwheels, had caught up to her.

Exhausted, Sally came to a stop. "I should have taken your bike." The words came between ragged, panting breaths. "Then you'd never have caught up to me."

"You've never ridden mine without falling," Emily remarked.

"This time I wouldn't have fallen."

"Then here," Emily said, shoving her bike in Sally's direction, "take it. Go just as far away as you want to go. You don't love any of us anymore. You don't love me."

"You wanted to be in a different tribe from me," Sally hurled back. "You wanted to be separate from me. This was no time to be separate from me." And then, to her surprise, she found herself sitting on the curb, her head down, her hands covering her face, sobbing out all the tears she hadn't cried since the day Mom had told them she had cancer.

Emily sat down next to Sally and put her arm around

her. "I didn't mean it," she said. "I know you love me. Just like I love you. I'm sorry about the tribes. I guess I was listening to other people. You know how they always say twins have to separate sooner or later. So I thought maybe this was the time."

Sally sniffled and wiped her nose with the back of her hand. "I think we're too young to separate. We can do that when we get to junior high."

"Well, maybe you're right," Emily said. "But I don't think we can do anything about it at camp. It's too late."

Sally nodded. "Yeah, I know. I mean, I made some friends in my tribe. It's not so bad, except everyone's fighting over who should be chief, and Angelo is going to win, and I don't like Angelo. No one does."

"Then how come he's going to win?" Emily asked.

"It's not an election, it's a contest," Sally explained. "And now, losing Claire—that's the last straw."

"Claire? The driver? I liked her," Emily agreed. "She told good stories. But she wasn't a good driver."

"She'd be a good drama counselor, though. Ruth said the camp might hire her. Only I can't find her. The bus company said they'd ask her to call me, but she hasn't called yet. Soon it'll be too late for that, too."

"I know where Claire lives," Emily said, as calmly

as if she were announcing that she liked mashed potatoes.

"What?" Sally turned and stared at her sister. "Why didn't you tell me?"

"I didn't know you wanted to know. You've got to admit that in the last five days you haven't said five words to me."

Sally scratched her head. It was true. "Let's forget that. Just tell me how you found out?"

"She told me."

How come Emily knew things about Claire that Sally didn't know? She'd thought *she* was the one who was Claire's special friend. "Why did she tell you?"

"Because I asked her. Remember that day I stayed out talking to her after you went in? I told her I had a friend who'd moved to Lenape, maybe she knew her. You remember Stacey LaFontaine. She lives on First Street near the Y. When I told that to Claire, she said she lived just a couple of blocks away on Third Street, but she didn't know the LaFontaines. And I said that was no surprise, because Lenape was quite big, much bigger than Watch Mountain, and I didn't know all the people in Watch Mountain. And so then she said . . ."

"That's great, Emily," Sally interrupted as she jumped to her feet. "That's just great. Let's bike over to Lenape and see if we can find her."

"That'll take an hour," Emily said. "We'd better go back and tell Mom where we're going."

"I don't think I can face Mom," Sally admitted.

"You'll have to, sooner or later. All you have to do is say you're sorry."

It was so easy for Emily. She saw her troubles as if they were etched in black and white. For Sally, every situation was a bundle of ifs, ands, and buts. "I don't think I can do that right now," she murmured.

"Then I'll tell her. You wait for me here."

Sally sat down again on the curb. Emily took a long time getting back. When she saw her, Sally understood why. She was carrying their lunch boxes. "I packed some cheese and crackers and fruit and cookies and soda," she said. "So we don't have to worry about getting home for supper. Mom said it was okay."

"She did?"

"Yeah. She said a long ride was a good idea." Emily smiled a little. "She said maybe it would give me time to straighten you out."

"Don't try," Sally warned.

"Don't worry. I won't. But I did tell her you felt terrible that you'd been so mean. I said you were very sorry."

"You did?"

"Yeah. Are you mad?"

Sally thought for a moment. "No. Maybe I'm even glad."

The road to Lenape was mostly downhill. Fortunately, there was a traffic signal at the corner of Ravencrest Road and the highway, or they'd have never made it across. In Lenape, they managed to avoid the really busy streets by following the bike route signs. The numbered streets began on the far side of Main Avenue. They'd been biking for an hour when they got to the YMCA on the corner of First Street and Elliot Road. They chained their bikes to the rack in front of the Y, then sat on a bench and ate their cheese and crackers.

When they'd finished, they remounted and rode over to Third Street, pausing at the corner of Third and Elliot. Sally looked up and down the long blocks. She saw rows of houses packed together, wide, wooden, two-story structures with porches and steps, most of them for two families at least.

Sally let out a long whistle. "We'll never find her. Five hundred people must live on each block. Can't you just see us knocking on every door? 'Does a fat lady named Claire live here?' They'll call the cops on us."

"We have a clue," Emily said. "Her house is yellow."

"How do you know?"

"She told me. She said she admired Petey's lavender house. She said hers was only yellow, but for Third Street, that was pretty good."

"I missed a really significant conversation," said Sally.

"You wouldn't have known it was significant at the time," Emily pointed out.

They started west on Third Street. Most of the houses were green upstairs and white down. A few were red and white. One was all gray. When they came upon one that was yellow and white, they walked up on the porch and inspected the names above the doorbells. Piskorowski and Doyle. "I don't know why we're looking," Emily said. "We don't know Claire's name or her daughter's name. I'll just ring the bell."

A young man wearing shorts and nothing else answered the door. "We're looking for our friend Claire," Emily said. "We forgot her house number. We know it's in the fifteen hundreds."

"She's kind of . . . well, kind of heavyset," Sally added.

"Sorry," the young man said. "She doesn't live here. Not upstairs at the Doyles', either." He pointed across the street. "A fat woman lives at fifteen sixty-five. I see her go in and out, but I don't know her name."

But 1565 was one of the green-and-whites. They thanked the shirtless man and continued on their way. The only other yellow-and-white house on the block yielded no better results. So they biked back to the corner and started east. "What does 'near the Y' mean?" Sally complained. "It could be anywhere within two miles. Or five miles. Everybody has a different idea of 'near.' "

"You get discouraged too easily," Emily said. "There aren't many yellow houses. We'll find her."

The next-to-the-last house on the block was yellow—not yellow and white, but all yellow. The downstairs bell was labeled Fitzgerald; the upstairs bell had two names, written one above the other, Connolly and Moresco. Sally rang the upstairs bell. She liked the name "Moresco." "Claire Moresco" sounded really nice. It sounded like a good name for an actress.

They heard footsteps clumping down the stairs. The door opened a crack. "My goodness, look who's here!" cried a deep, rich voice. The voice's owner undid the chain and threw the door open wide. It was Claire.

S E V E N

"Come on in," Claire said. "I was just about to call you."

"You were?" Sally said.

"Yes. I was away for a couple of days, at a friend's. You know, recuperating from losing my job." Claire gestured for the girls to follow her up the stairs. Despite her size, she reached the top quickly. Sally and Emily were right behind her. "I got home this afternoon, and there was this message from the bus company to call you. What's up?"

She led them into a combination bedroom and sitting room filled with books, plants, embroidered cushions, and colored snapshots. On the desk was a black-and-white portrait of a glamorous young woman in a satin evening gown. It took Sally a few minutes to realize it was a photograph of Claire herself in her Hollywood starlet days.

Claire invited them to sit on two large cushions on the floor. She took the room's only real seat—a worn, comfortable club chair with a large, matching ottoman.

"Do you have a Shakespeare book here?" Sally asked.

"Sure," said Claire. She hoisted herself out of the chair, pulled a volume from the shelf, handed it to Sally, and sat down again.

"Hey!" Sally exclaimed. "This is exactly the same book we have at home." She found the picture of the magician and the monster and showed it to Claire. "Tell us this story," she demanded.

"*The Tempest?* Was that the big emergency? You needed me to tell you *The Tempest?*"

"Oh, no," Sally said. "What we need is a drama counselor at camp. That's why I was trying to find you. Will you be our drama counselor, please, Claire?"

Claire's eyes widened. Her mouth opened, then closed again. Although in general not the silent type, she seemed for the moment surprised into speechlessness.

"We think you'd be very good," Emily said. "Sally asked the head counselor about it. She said she'd like to talk to you."

"She could pay you," Sally said. "Not much, but

something." She stared at Claire with great concentration, willing her to say yes.

In a moment, Claire had recovered sufficiently to speak. "You don't have to talk me into it. I'd love to do it. I don't know if I can, but I'd sure like to try. Do you really think they'll have me? I worked at a day-care center once. I did a bit of drama with my kids. Maybe that counts as a little experience."

"When you talk to Ruth," Emily said, "make it sound like a lot of experience."

"I loved doing it," Claire said. "I'd really like to try again."

"I don't see why you ever even took a job driving a van," Sally said.

Claire shook her head. "It never occurred to me to look for a job doing drama with kids," she said. "I wouldn't have known where to begin the search. I can't work in a school. I never took any education courses."

"You were an actress," Sally reminded her. "That ought to count for something."

"Will you call Ruth tomorrow?" Emily asked.

"First thing," Claire assured her.

"Good," Sally said. "Now can you tell us *The Tempest?*"

"It's the least I can do," Claire agreed. "First, I'll get you something to eat." She left the room for a few minutes and returned carrying a tray of Cokes and corn chips. Sally and Emily munched while they listened; Claire munched at appropriate pauses, giving her words, uttered in her rich, musical voice, time to sink in.

Prospero was the duke of Milan, Claire told them. With the help of the king of Naples, Prospero's brother, Antonio, threw Prospero out and took over the dukedom. Antonio and the king set Prospero and his baby daughter, Miranda, adrift in a little boat, sure that they would never be heard from again.

Eventually the boat washed up on a magical island. Prospero, already a learned man, now had time to become a master magician. The fantastic creatures of the island became his servants. One was Ariel, a beautiful airy spirit. Another was the deformed, ugly, earthbound monster, Caliban.

When Miranda was sixteen, a ship carrying, among others, Antonio, the king of Naples, and the king's son, Ferdinand, sailed close to the island. Prospero called up a great storm, and the ship was wrecked. No one was killed, but everyone was washed up on different parts of the island and thought the others were dead.

Ferdinand came upon Prospero's cave, where he fell in love with Miranda the moment he laid eyes on her. Other than her father, Ferdinand was the first man Miranda had ever seen. She was amazed. "O brave new world," she said, "that has such people in't!" She promptly fell in love with him, too. Prospero, however, made Ferdinand prove his love for Miranda by setting him to hard labor.

Meanwhile, Ariel, acting under Prospero's instructions, arranged strange and troubling adventures for the other shipwrecked passengers. At last Prospero felt that his enemies had suffered enough. He ordered Ariel to lead them to his cave, where each learned that the others were alive. The king agreed to the marriage of his son and Miranda, Antonio and Prospero were reconciled, and Prospero decided to return to Milan and his rightful position as duke, leaving his marvelous island forever. His final instruction to Ariel was to arrange fair winds for their journey home. Then he set the spirit free.

"That was so different from the others," Emily said when the story was over.

Sally sighed. "It was a fairy tale, a wonderful fairy tale."

"If I were an artist, I would draw pictures for that story," Emily said. "But I'm not."

"Draw them, anyway," Claire suggested.

"They won't come out like I imagine."

"I bet even Shakespeare felt his plays didn't live up to his dreams," Claire replied. "That didn't stop him."

For a moment no one spoke. Sally was still lost in the story. "You know, Claire," she said at last, "I wanted to find you to tell you there was a chance for you to get a job at camp. But that was only one reason. The other reason was what you said—to get you to tell me *The Tempest*. It's like I need those stories. Everything's so lousy, I need those stories."

"You mean because your mom has cancer?" Claire said.

Sally nodded.

"You should have seen my two grandsons when their mother had cancer. They absolutely turned into wild men. They drove me crazy."

"Sally has turned into a wild man," Emily said.

"I have not!" Sally exclaimed. "I'm the same as I've always been."

Emily merely raised her eyebrows.

Sally sprang to another line of defense. "Maybe I feel things more than you do," she said. "You roll with the punches, and I can't do that."

Emily jumped to her feet. "Just because I try to make things easier for everybody by acting nice, you think I don't have feelings? My God, Sally, how can you be so dumb? We've been twins for eleven years. More than eleven if you count the time we were together in Mom's belly, and you still don't know a thing about me."

"You don't know a thing about me, either," Sally retorted.

Emily turned to Claire. "Thank you for the refreshments," she said. "I hope I see you at camp. Good-bye." She turned back to Sally, glared at her, then ran out of the room.

Sally remained rooted to the floor. "It wasn't always like this," she told Claire. "We used to be close. This afternoon, on the hill, I thought we were getting back together. I guess I was wrong."

"Not wrong," said Claire. "Hurry up—go after her."

Sally didn't move.

"Don't you understand what she was telling you?" Claire asked. "You and she are feeling the same things. You may be acting different, but you're not feeling different. Hurry up. Go after her." She stood up, reached for Sally's hand, and pulled her to her feet.

Sally clattered down the stairs, but by the time she reached the front porch, Emily and her bike had disappeared. Sally knew she'd never catch up. She had the whole long ride home, most of it uphill, to think about what Claire had said. Could Claire be right? Was Emily really as miserable as Sally herself was? She wondered now if she'd ever find out.

At home, Dad and Lisa were in the family room watching TV. "Where's Mom?" Sally asked.

"Gone to bed," Lisa said. "You knocked her out."

Sally bit her lip to prevent herself from snapping back. She turned to her father. "Do you think she's asleep? Can I go see her?"

Dad's eyes held hers for a long moment. "Knock very softly," he said at last. "If she's asleep, she won't hear you. If she's awake, she will, and you can go in."

Upstairs, Sally heard the murmur of TV voices coming from both her room and her mother's room. She knocked gently on her mother's door. "Who is it?" Mom asked.

"Sally."

"Come in."

Mom wasn't in bed. She was wearing her night-gown and a cotton robe, but she was sitting in the chair watching TV. She pressed the mute button on the remote control. The light continued to flicker, but the sound had ceased.

"What is it, Sally?"

"I'm sorry, Mom," Sally said. "I hope you have a wonderful time at the beach." She swallowed hard. "I'm glad you're going."

Mom smiled. "Thank you, Sally. Thank you very much for saying that. Come here." Her mother held out her arms. In a moment, Sally was locked in her mother's embrace. "I love you so very much. Good night, my darling. Sleep tight," Mom said.

"Good night, Mom. You sleep tight, too."

In the twins' room, Emily was also watching TV. Maybe for the rest of the family, television was like the Shakespeare stories were for Sally—an escape from their troubles. Though the Shakespeare stories were more than that. As Claire had once said, they taught you about life, too. Sally wasn't sure TV did that. Well, maybe sometimes. It depended on the program.

Emily didn't say anything when Sally came in. She didn't even look up. Sally walked over to the TV set and reached for the on-off button. Then she changed her mind and just turned down the volume.

Emily finally deigned to notice her. "Hey, what's the big idea?"

"This will only take a minute. I want to talk to you." Sally sat down on Emily's bed. "I just want to say I'm sorry. I know you feel as bad as I do. I'm sorry I said you didn't. It was a dumb thing to say."

"Yeah, it was," Emily agreed. "Okay. I'm glad you said that. Thank you. Now can I hear the rest of 'The Wonder Years'?" With a sigh, Sally returned to the TV set. "You can watch, too, if you want to," Emily added brightly.

Sally plopped down on her bed. She supposed she'd gotten as much as she could expect. She did feel a little better. At least the ocean that had separated her and Emily seemed to have shrunk. It was more like a Great Lake now. But although she and Emily might be feeling the same things, no one had said what those things were. No one could. They were too terrible to say, like monsters no one wanted to let out of their caves. So although Sally felt a little better, she didn't feel all better. A stone still lay on her heart.

A two-point swimming race that Angelo won easily made him the chief of the Apache tribe. "I won!" he cried. "I won fair and square. Right, Marty? Right?"

Marty didn't say anything.

Angelo glared at him. "Right?"

"Yeah. Right." Marty picked up his towel and started back toward the tent.

"This is impossible," Sally told him. "We have to do something to change it."

"There's nothing you can do now," Marty replied.

"You're going to take this lying down?" Sally protested.

"Like Angelo said, he won fair and square."

"Boy, he's obnoxious."

"He's disgusting," Marty added.

At lunchtime, the whole tribe, except for Gerald, sat around outside the tent eating their sandwiches. Gerald was fetching supplies from the arts and crafts tent. He'd picked this time to go because he knew Amy and the Seminoles would be there.

"So," Marty asked, "what are we going to do for the powwow?"

"We're going to do something super," said Angelo. "Something really, really good. We're going to build a tepee."

He looked around as if he expected cheers, but the only one to comment was Sally. "We can't build a tepee. The Senecas are building a teepee."

"How do you know?"

"My sister told me."

"We'll build a better tepee."

"But that's dumb," Sally said. "It's dumb to do the same thing as the Senecas when we know they're doing it. You have to think of something else."

"I'm the chief," Angelo shouted, "and I get to pick. We're building a tepee."

"Building a tepee *is* kind of dumb," Marty said mildly. "I mean if we actually know the Senecas are doing it."

"You're just a sore loser," Angelo shot back.

"Are you going to let that jerk get away with calling you names?" Sally asked.

"Well, no, of course not." Marty leaned forward so that his forehead was almost touching Angelo's. "I don't give a darn about being chief. You were the one who was so worried we'd look stupid at the powwow. What could be stupider than doing the same thing as the Senecas?"

"That's right, Marty," Sally cried. "You tell him."

Angelo jumped to his feet and landed a kick to Marty's chest, which sent him sprawling in the dirt. But Marty was up in an instant, with his fists raised. He shot for Angelo's jaw, but Angelo turned in time, and the punch landed on his shoulder. The two of them danced around, ducking and punching, punching and ducking. First one would land a blow, and then the other. Their punches grew harder and harder as the two of them grew angrier and angrier.

"Come on, Marty," Sally shouted. "Get him!"

"That's it, Angelo," Gil screamed. "Do it again, Angelo."

Sally was screeching like a mad woman. The other kids, standing in a ring around the fighters, shouted and screamed, too, cheering on one or the other. Sally knew they were all acting crazy, but none of them, including she herself, seemed able to stop.

Except for Melanie, who suddenly seized Sally's arm. "Cut out the yelling," she exclaimed. "We'd better break up this fight. One of them is going to end up with a bloody nose or a black eye. Where's that Gerald? Isn't it just like him to disappear when we need him most."

They both turned. At the bottom of the hill, Sally saw Gerald on the dirt path. A large, white-haired woman was walking beside him. She recognized Claire immediately.

Melanie tore down the hill, "You better hurry up," she called to them. "Angelo and Marty are killing each other."

Gerald and Claire quickened their pace, but Angelo and Marty must have heard Melanie's shouts, too. By the time Gerald and Claire reached the Apache tent, the two boys had collapsed on the ground. Their hair was hanging in their eyes, their white T-shirts were stained with dust and grass, their faces streaked with tears and dirt. "What's going on here?" Gerald asked.

Angelo and Marty said nothing. "They had a fight," Melanie explained.

"Who started it?" Gerald wanted to know.

"He did," the two boys muttered simultaneously.

"Does it matter who started it?" Claire asked. "The important thing is that it's stopped—and that it's not going to happen again."

Maxie stared at the newcomer. "Who are you?" he asked.

"I'm Claire," she replied. "I'm your new drama counselor. You want to do some drama?"

"Right now?" Gil asked.

Claire nodded.

"Not much," Maxie replied. "The plays we do in school are silly."

"How about the rest of you?" Claire asked.

No one replied.

Claire pointed to Sally and Maxie. "You two," she said, "show me what happened just now. Act it out."

"You mean between Marty and Angelo?" Sally asked.

"Yes." She turned to Maxie again. "What's your name?"

He told her.

"Maxie, you look pretty clever. You be Marty. And Sally, you be Angelo."

Sally threw back her head, folded her arms across her chest, and strutted over to Gil. "Now that I'm chief, I'm really God, and I'm going to tell you what we're going to do for the powwow," she thundered. "We're going to put up a tepee." She put enormous emphasis on the last syllable. Melanie giggled, and so did several others.

Maxie was not to be outdone by Sally. He rubbed his nose with his finger the way Marty did twenty times a day. Again everyone laughed. Inspired, Maxie managed to exaggerate the barely noticeable twang in Marty's speech. "Tha-a-t's stu-u-pid. The Senecas are gonna put up a tepee."

In a few moments the whole drama unfolded, if not in an entirely accurate version. After all, no one was playing Sally. So carried away were she and Maxie by their parts that when they got to the fight, they lifted their fists, ready to haul off and sock each other.

"Okay," said Claire. "Very good. You can stop now. We get the point."

Everyone clapped, even Marty and Angelo. "That was a play, Maxie," Claire said. "I don't think it was stupid. Do you?"

"It wasn't like the plays we put on in school," Maxie replied.

"What we're going to do here is probably nothing like what you do at school. It's games, at least to start with. You want to try?"

Claire sorted them into pairs. For the first game, one of each pair was blindfolded while the other led him or her around obstacles. Then they switched. Claire made Marty lead Angelo and Angelo lead Marty.

Next she told the pairs that one had to be a screaming toddler and the other an embarrassed parent in a crowded restaurant. They had to improvise what happened.

For the third game, Claire gave each pair a paper bag containing three weird objects. Sally and Gil got an eye dropper, a Garfield doll, and a dead spider. They had to work out stories using the objects in their bags. Some of the stories were so wild, Sally laughed until her sides hurt. She couldn't remember when she'd last laughed so hard.

After Claire left to work with another tribe, Sally realized she hadn't once thought about home for the entire hour. She'd actually forgotten her mother's whole trip to the beach. Playing theater games was as good as Shakespeare stories—maybe even better.

But as soon as she remembered that she wasn't thinking about Mom, Mom was all she could think of. How could she have a good time when maybe her mother had pulled over on the side of the road, vomiting out her guts. She ought to be thinking about her mother every single second, praying all the time that she'd get cured, whether God was listening or not.

E I G H T

Acouple of days later, Claire asked them to improvise a play around a story they all knew. "*Macbeth!*" Marty shouted. "That's the story we should do. Only first you better tell it to us again, Sally, because we might not remember it all."

"Oh, no," Sally said. "Let Claire tell it. I heard it from her. She tells it much better than I do."

But Claire refused, and Sally had to do it. Then the Apaches worked out their own version. Angelo played Macbeth, Maxie was King Duncan, and Marty was Macduff. But their version didn't take place in medieval Scotland. It took place at Camp Wampum, and the three guys were struggling over the chiefdom of the Minnehaha tribe. Melanie, Gil, and Brian were the witches—only they weren't really witches, they were gypsy fortune-tellers living in trailers near the camp. Sally was Lady Macbeth.

Since there were only ten Apaches, most of them had to play several parts. They whipped behind trees to take off a hat or put on a pair of sunglasses, then came out again as some other character. They kept interrupting the action to throw ideas at one another about what should happen next. They were nowhere near the end of the story when their hour with Claire was up.

"We'll have to finish this tomorrow," she said.

"We should polish it up real good," Maxie said, "and do it for the powwow."

"Maxie!" Angelo cried. "We're building a tepee for the powwow. Remember?"

"We've never even practiced tepee building," Maxie said. "No one wants to."

"Macbeth is not Indian," Angelo announced firmly.

"But our version is about a camp," Sally pointed out. "It's about a tribe." She shoved her index finger into Angelo's chest. "And you're the chief, Angelo. You've got the leading part. You're the star."

"That's just it," Angelo said. "I *am* the chief. And I say we're building a tepee. We'll build it ten times better and ten times faster than the Senecas."

"How can we if we've never done it, not even once?" Melanie wondered.

"Cliff Breakwater will tell me what we need to get

for tepee building," Angelo replied. "We'll start prac-
ticing tomorrow."

"No one wants to," Maxie repeated.

"You will," Angelo said. "If you don't want to look
like fools at the powwow, you will."

"But the play is so much fun," said Marty.

"You lost, Marty," Angelo reminded him. "I'm the
chief. So we do what I say."

Sally was sorry the Apaches hadn't turned into a
real tribe, as she had once hoped they would. She
didn't want to build a tepee any more than Marty or
Maxie or Melanie. But at least they were all having
fun with *Macbeth*. Even Angelo seemed to be enjoying it. Maybe something would happen to change his
mind.

Mom got home from the beach Thursday night. Her
cheeks were pink and her skin was lightly tanned.
She hadn't looked so well since before the operation.
Sally expected her to be bubbling over with stories
about the friends she'd been with, the shops she'd
visited, the time she'd spent with Aunt Lou, Uncle
Andrew, Jenny and Jake. But instead she was very
quiet.

"What's the matter, Mom?" Lisa asked. "Don't you
feel good?"

"I feel fine," she replied. "I guess I'm just a little
nervous."

"About what?"

"Tomorrow."

"What's happening tomorrow?" Sally wanted to know.

"Don't you remember?" Lisa snapped. "The chemo."

"The effect of it is kind of cumulative," Mom said. "I feel a little sicker each time." She hugged herself, as if on this hot August night she felt a chill. "Oh, but it's really not so bad," she added quickly. "I worry too much in advance. The anticipation is worse than the reality."

Sally didn't believe it. Mom was just saying that to make them feel better.

After dinner, Mom helped clean up, then watched TV in the family room for a little while. But she kept getting up to change the station, even though she could have done it with the remote. Sally didn't say anything, even if she was enjoying the program, and neither did anyone else. But no one left to watch TV in another room, either.

"God, all these programs are so stupid," Mom finally exclaimed. "And every two seconds, there's another commercial. I really can't bear it another minute."

"Shall I go out and get a video?" Dad asked.

"No," Mom returned sharply. "Mostly they're stupid, too. The entertainment industry in this country has sunk to a new low." She snapped off the machine and went upstairs. In a few minutes, Dad followed her.

"Boy, is she ever cross," Sally said. "What's with her?"

"She told you, dumbo," Lisa said. "She's cross for the same reason she was so quiet at dinner. Can't you understand that?"

"Yes, I can," Sally said. "But I sure don't have to like it."

"No one likes it," Lisa agreed quietly. "Especially Mom."

When Sally and Emily climbed out of the van the next morning, Claire was waiting for them in the parking lot. "Hey, guys," she said, "you want to have dinner at my house tonight? It'll give you a chance to meet the wild men."

"The wild men?" Emily queried.

"My grandsons. Actually, you'll like them. I think you'll like my daughter, too. I'm making a couple of soufflés. My soufflés are wonderful."

"I love soufflés," Emily said. "Mom used to make them before she had to worry about Dad's high cholesterol."

"Will you tell another Shakespeare story?" Sally asked.

"Sure," said Claire. "Your pick."

"*Hamlet,* I think," Sally replied. The *Hamlet* picture in the Shakespeare book was pretty interesting. It showed a man dressed all in black staring at a skull in his hand. The caption read, "Alas! poor Yorick. I knew him, Horatio, a fellow of infinite jest." Sally wanted to know who Yorick was, and who Horatio was—and who Hamlet was, for that matter.

"We'll have to ask if we can go out for dinner when we get home," Emily said.

"I'm sure it'll be all right," Sally added. "We'll call you right away."

"And then I'll come over and pick you up," said Claire.

"We could ride our bikes," Emily suggested.

Sally shot Claire a sidelong glance. "We don't want you to get lost."

"You cannot ride your bikes home in the dark. I will not get lost." Claire made her voice stern, but she had to work hard to keep the corners of her mouth from turning up. "I will pick you up, and I will take you back."

Sally was so excited at the idea of having dinner with Claire that she hardly gave her mother's chemo treatment a single thought all day. When they arrived home in the late afternoon, Mom didn't seem too bad. Instead of lying in bed, she was reclining in a chaise on the porch, reading a magazine. "Maybe I was wrong," she said cheerfully. "Maybe what really happens with chemo is you get used to it. Or maybe those few days at the beach just did me a lot of good. I really feel okay today after all."

"That's great," Emily said.

"Your dad will be home soon," Mom continued. "He's getting out of work early. Lisa'll be home soon, too. He and I have a super surprise for the three of you."

"What is it?" Emily asked immediately.

"I promised I wouldn't tell until he got home."

"Come on, Mom," Sally said. "You've told us this much, you have to tell us the rest."

"I haven't told you anything," Mom replied, grinning.

"I have something to tell *you*," said Sally. "Emily and I are going out to dinner. Isn't that nice? Claire invited us. She said she'll pick us up and take us home. She's making soufflés."

"It certainly was nice of her to ask you," Mom said. "Awfully nice. But you'll have to call her and tell her you'll come another night."

Sally felt her body stiffen. "What's wrong with tonight?"

"That's the surprise. I guess I'll just have to tell you."

"Yeah," Sally said. "You better."

"You're going to the shore. As soon as Lisa gets home, Grandma and Grandpa will come over to drive you down. You'll stay at a motel near Jenny and Jake and spend the whole weekend on the beach with them."

"Fantastic!" Emily cried. "I'm going up to pack right now."

"But what about Claire?" Sally said. "It's kind of crummy to disappoint her after she's gone to the trouble of making extra soufflés."

"We told her we'd have to ask," Emily returned. "She knew we couldn't promise until we'd asked."

"That's right," Mom said. "She'll understand. You don't have to worry about that, Sally. You can just go to the beach and have fun with Jenny and Jake. It's what you've wanted to do all summer."

"But it's not what I want to do tonight," Sally announced firmly. "I want to go to Claire's. Let Emily and Lisa go. I'll just stay home."

Emily turned and stared at her. "Are you crazy? You'd give up a whole weekend at the beach just to have dinner with Claire?"

"Yes. I love Claire."

"Well, I like her, too, but . . ."

"I love her."

Emily shook her head. "You *are* crazy. She's not even a relative."

"Girls, sit down, please," Mom said. "I need to talk to you." Emily and Sally planted themselves side by side on the other chaise. "You have to go to the beach. The beach did me so much good. I realized I've just been hanging around the house too much.

So Dad and I are going to New York for the weekend. We need some time by ourselves. We need to talk about something else besides kids and doctors and medicine." She sat up straight and put her feet on the floor. "We'll go to the theater and eat in restaurants and not think about anything but enjoying ourselves—which we'll be able to do because you'll be enjoying yourselves, too."

"Hey, listen, I have an idea," Sally said. "Why can't we go down tomorrow morning? If you're leaving tonight, we can sleep at Grandma and Grandpa's, or they can sleep here."

"Grandpa isn't spending the weekend with you," Mom said. "He's just driving you down and picking you up Sunday. Tomorrow he has to be with a client who's in some kind of trouble. He's driving all the way down to the shore and all the way back, and all the way down again and all the way back, just so you guys can have some fun. That's some kind of grandfather."

"He sure is," Emily agreed. "Can I go pack now?"

"Oh, yes," said Mom. "You, too, Sally."

"I'm not packing," Sally said, "because I'm not going. I'll find a friend to stay with—Petey maybe, or Gloria. Or maybe I'll ask Claire if I can spend the whole weekend with her."

"Four people live in that little apartment already," said Emily. "There's no room for you."

"Sally, I don't understand you," Mom said. "All

summer long you've been bitching, bitching, bitching because you couldn't go to the beach. And now you have your chance and you don't want to go."

"I don't understand *you*, Mom," Sally returned. "How could you make plans for us without even asking us first?"

"I never dreamed you wouldn't want to go." Mom shook her head in a kind of weary amazement. "It never even occurred to me."

"You made us go to camp," Sally shot back. "Now I like camp. Now I like the people at camp. And now you're trying to take that away from me."

"What are you talking about?" Mom's eyes blazed, the way they did when she got really angry. "Monday you'll be back at camp. Nobody's taking anything away from you."

"You're taking dinner with Claire away from me," Sally insisted.

"You know what I think?" Mom said. "I think you're just being contrary, and I don't understand why. This summer of all summers, I thought you'd try to cooperate. Something's happened to you, Sally. You're not the girl I thought you were."

It seemed to Sally they'd gone over this ground before, not once, but a dozen times. "You keep saying that," she said. "It's a horrid thing to say."

Her mother's voice was cold and flat. "If the shoe fits, wear it. Now get yourself upstairs and pack." She rose from her seat and went inside. Emily went with her. But Sally stayed right where she was. They couldn't make her pack. And unless they threw her into the car bodily and tied her down, they couldn't make her go, either. She was going to have dinner at Claire's. She was, even if it was the last meal she ate on this earth.

When Dad and Lisa came home a short while later, they found Sally still stewing on the back porch. "What's the matter with you?" Lisa said. "You look like you just had a fight with your only friend."

"When she hears the news, she'll cheer up in a minute," Dad said.

"No I won't." Sally spit out her words.

"Oh, you will," Dad said. "Come in. We'll find Mom and then we'll tell you about the surprise."

"I know what the surprise is. Mom had to tell me, because Emily and I had made a dinner date with Claire."

"Claire?" Dad wondered.

"Our drama counselor. She invited us over. I'm not going to the shore. I'm going to Claire's."

The screen door swung open, and Mom stood in the doorway. "Young lady," she said to Sally, "I thought I told you to go upstairs and pack. Now get a move on."

"Lynnie, what's going on here?" Dad asked.

Mom turned. "Hi, Bart. Hello, Lisa. We're having a problem with Sally."

"I'm not going. I told you, I'm not going. I'll stay

with Petey or Gloria." Sally slid off the lounge. "I'll go in and call them right now."

"Mom and Dad plan this great weekend for us, and you don't want to go?" Lisa said. "You're crazy."

That was the second sister who'd called her crazy. "You're crazy if you think I'm crazy," she cried.

"You've been acting strange all summer," said Dad.

His voice was mild, but his remark hit Sally like a wasp's sting. "You're the ones who've been acting strange. You and Mom."

"But Mom's sick," Dad said. "You know that. And instead of helping, you've been making things worse."

"If she's so sick, how could she go to the shore? How can she go to New York?" Sally shouted. "She can go where she wants. She can do what she wants. But I can't. It isn't fair, and you know it."

Dad's eyes popped, as if someone had just hit him in the belly. He lifted his hand as if he were about to hit back. But the only time he'd struck Sally in all her life was when, at the age of two, she'd run into the road. Instead he seized her upper arm and held it so tightly that she couldn't move. "Get upstairs and pack," he said. "And don't come back down until I call you."

He let her go then, and she stumbled through the door, tears streaming down her cheeks. She sobbed all the way up the stairs. In her room, she threw herself facedown on her bed and kept right on sobbing.

Emily dropped the T-shirt she was pulling out of her drawer and sat down on the bed next to her. "Sally, what's the matter? Why are you crying?"

"You know why," Sally mumbled into the pillow.

"I can't understand what you're saying."

Sally lifted her head. "Leave me alone," she shouted. Once more she buried her head.

"Okay," Emily said. She stood up, picked the T-shirt out of the drawer again, and laid it in her knapsack. Minutes passed. The only sounds in the room were Sally's sniffles and the opening and closing of Emily's bureau drawers.

The door to the bedroom stood ajar, but someone was knocking on it, anyway. It couldn't be Mom or Dad or Lisa. They'd just walk in. Though she knew she must look like a wrung-out dishrag, Sally sat up to see who it was.

Emily saw the visitor first. "Oh, Claire!" she exclaimed. "No one called to tell you we couldn't come. I'm terribly sorry, really, I am."

"Don't worry about it, Emily," Claire assured her. "It's no big thing. We'll make it another time." She glanced at Sally. "Your folks said I could come up and talk to you."

"I'm going back with you," Sally said. "Could I stay over at your house?"

"No, Sally," Claire replied softly. "I'm sorry, but you can't."

"I hate it here," Sally said. "I absolutely hate it."

"But here is where you are," Claire said. "Here is where you have to be." She sat down on Emily's bed. The mattress and spring sunk like a hammock under her weight.

"I'd rather be anywhere else," Sally said. "I'd rather be at your house. I'd rather be at camp. I'd rather be in Illyria. I'd rather be on Prospero's island. I'd even rather be in Scotland when Macbeth was king."

"Do you remember what happens to Prospero at the end of *The Tempest?*" Claire asked.

Sally took a tissue from the box on the night table and blew her nose. "Sure. He goes back to Milan."

Claire nodded. "Even Prospero has to leave his magic island. Even he has to return to the real world."

"So?"

"Camp is great. Stories are great. Vacations are great. But you have to live in this house with these people."

"No, I don't," Sally insisted. "There are lots of places I can go." But she knew even as she uttered them that her words were nonsense.

Since she'd greeted Claire, Emily had not spoken. That didn't mean she hadn't been listening. She turned away from her bureau and marched over to the bed where Sally and Claire were sitting. "We used to talk in this house," she said. "When we had a problem, we used to sit down and talk about it. We used to tell how we felt."

"I just did," said Sally. "I told how I felt, and they got so mad I thought they were going to kill me."

"You didn't tell them what's really bothering you," Emily said.

Sally stared at her sister. "Well, Miss Smarty-Pants, if you know so much, what really is bothering me?" she snapped.

Emily sat down between Sally and Claire. "You're scared," she said. "You're scared out of your mind. And so am I."

Sally sighed. It was almost a sigh of relief. Emily knew.

At first, Sally was surprised about that. And then, when she thought about it, she wasn't. For eleven years, each of them had almost always known what the other one was feeling, even if they were only fraternal twins, and even if, as sometimes happened, they didn't feel the same. They'd disagreed before, but this summer was the first time a real chasm had opened between them. The really surprising thing was that after the day they'd biked to Claire's house, Sally still hadn't guessed that Emily was just as scared as she was.

"What are you scared of?" Claire asked.

Emily's voice dropped to a whisper. "We're scared our mom's going to die." She looked at Sally.

Sally nodded slowly. "So what's the use of talking? We can't say that."

"Of course you can say that," Claire said. "You have to say that."

"I'm scared of something else, too," Sally said. "I'm scared *I'm* going to die." She looked back at Emily. "Are you?"

"Well, I wasn't until you told me about breast cancer being hereditary. So now I am."

Sally shrugged. "You see? I talk too much."

"No," said Claire. "What's really happened is that you've stopped talking. All of you have, I guess. You're tiptoeing around each other like you're walking on glass. Or else you scream at each other over things that don't really matter, things that are just taking the place of what does matter. That's what happened to us when my daughter had cancer. We finally went to see a family therapist. It helped us a lot."

"Do you think that's what we should do?" Sally asked.

"I don't know. Each family is different. My daughter's cancer showed up just a few months after her husband left. The people in her house were never very good at talking to each other. Maybe they weren't any good at it in my house, either."

"We used to be," Emily said. "We should try it again."

"Oh, my God," Sally said. "If we tell Mom we think she may die, and we think we may die, that'll be the end. Really, it will be."

"No," said Claire. "Trust me. It'll be the beginning."

N I N E

Downstairs, Claire kissed first Emily on the cheek and then Sally. "You can have dinner at my house some other time—if it's all right with your folks."

"It'll be all right," Mom said.

"Good. Well, so long now. Good luck." Claire left. The kitchen door and then the porch door slammed behind her.

"That's a nice lady," Dad said.

"Are you all packed?" Mom asked.

"Let's sit down," Emily said. "We have to talk."

"There's no time," Mom said. Like a little girl, she was twisting a lock of hair around her finger. "We can talk some other day."

As if a bolt of lightning had suddenly shot through black clouds, the landscape of her mother's mind was illuminated for Sally. Her mother was scared, too. She was the most scared of all. "Please, Mom," Sally begged very softly, "please, can't we talk now?"

Lisa sat down at the kitchen table. They'd always had family conferences at the kitchen table. Dad sat down next. Then Emily sat down.

Mom stared at Sally. Slowly she pulled out her chair. She and Sally sat down at the same time. "So what is it, Sally?" she asked. "What do you want to say?"

Her eyes on the table, Sally shook her head.

"Now, after you got us here, all of a sudden you're tongue-tied?" Dad snapped.

"That's not too useful, is it, Dad?" Lisa said quietly. "I mean, if you really do want Sally to tell us what's on her mind."

Startled, Sally looked up. She felt tears rise again at the back of her eyes, but they were not the same kind of tears she'd cried before. She blinked hard and managed a small smile at Lisa.

"Okay, Lisa," said Dad. "I get you. Let's start all over again. What's bothering you, Sally? I mean, what's *really* bothering you?"

"Emily is worried, too," Sally said.

"Worried about what?" The flatness had gone out of her mother's voice; the old familiar warmth had returned.

Sally lifted her eyes to her mother's. "We're worried that you're going to die."

For a long moment, their eyes held. Then Mom

said gently, "You know what, Sally? I worry about that, too. But only sometimes. Most of the time, I know I'm *not* going to die. I mean, of course I'm going to die, but not anytime soon."

"Another thing," Sally went on, her voice so soft her mother had to lean toward her to hear it. "I worry that I'm going to die. Breast cancer is hereditary, you know."

"Then where did I get it?" Mom asked. "My mother never had it, and neither did hers. Just because I have it doesn't mean you're necessarily going to get it."

"But we might," said Lisa.

"You mean you think about this, too?" Sally exclaimed.

"What do you think I am?" Lisa retorted. "Some kind of robot?"

Slowly Sally shook her head. She'd been so wrapped up in her own fury that she hadn't known what Lisa was feeling, she hadn't known what her mother was feeling, she hadn't even known what her own twin was feeling. The funny part was, they were all feeling the same. They were behaving differently but feeling the same. Somehow, that made things better. It cured the loneliness.

"Any woman *might* get breast cancer," Mom said.

"But our chances are greater," Lisa said. "You know that's true."

Mom sighed. "I feel so guilty about that."

"Guilty?" Dad cried. "You didn't get breast cancer on purpose."

"Sometimes I get so angry at you, Mom," said Sally. "As if you *had* gotten it on purpose. I know that's stupid, but that's how I feel sometimes. Can you understand something as terrible as that?"

"Oh, Sally, can I ever. Because I get mad at myself, too."

"For what?" Emily asked.

"For having breast cancer."

"But, Mom . . ."

"Yes," Mom said, "I know. It's just as dumb as you kids getting mad at me. But I can't help it. I'm mad at myself for not being able to control my own stupid body. I have to get over that, of course. I have to admit that I'm not Superwoman. That's the hardest part."

"Do you ever get angry, Dad?" Sally asked.

"Didn't I just get so mad at you I almost hit you?" Dad said.

"I mean at Mom," Sally said.

Dad glanced at Mom. "Tell them what happened last night," he said.

Mom leaned forward and dropped her voice. "He got so mad because his good jacket was missing a button that I thought he was going to divorce me. And I've never been any kind of a mender. He's known that for seventeen years."

"You know the real reason I was mad at your mother," Dad added quietly. "It wasn't because she hadn't sewn the button on my jacket."

"It's because she has cancer," Sally said.

"And sometimes I can't do all the things I used to do," Mom said. "But sometimes I can."

Dad shot her one of their private smiles. "I know," he said. Then he turned back to Sally. "So you see, I'm no better than the rest of you. We each show it differently, that's all."

"You know, kids," Mom said, "you ought to talk to my oncologist."

"Dr. Ghardelli?" Emily asked.

"Yes. My cancer doctor. The one who gives me the chemotherapy."

"The torturer," Sally said.

"It doesn't hurt to get the chemo," Mom said. "It goes in with a pinprick."

Sally put her head in her hands. "If only all of this hadn't happened."

"But it has happened," Dad said, "and we have to deal with it. I think we are dealing with it."

"At last," Emily murmured. Sally was the only one who heard her. Dad thought Sally had forced this discussion, but Sally knew it was really Emily's doing. Emily always had been very good at organizing things. It was she, really, who'd organized the Four Seasons Club they had with Jenny, Jake, and Aunt Nan.

"Dr. Ghardelli knows so much," Mom continued. "And she's very nice. She could answer all of your questions. Will you talk to her? People have a lot of funny ideas about cancer. She'll set you straight."

"Can't we just ask you?" said Emily.

"Oh, there's so much I don't know," Mom replied. "And some things I don't want to know, I guess," she added softly.

She doesn't want us to ask her what her chances of dying really are, Sally thought. She wants us to ask Dr. Ghardelli. "Okay," Sally announced briskly. "We'll go see Doctor Ghardelli. Will you arrange it?"

Mom nodded. "And I'll drive you over, too. If I can work up the courage, maybe I'll even stay with you while you meet with her."

They sat at the table talking for such a long time that it got to be too late to drive to the beach. Grandma and Grandpa picked up pizza and brought it over for supper—not their usual Friday night dinner, but Mom lit the candles and Dad sang the blessing over the wine, anyway. The kids never went to the shore at all. Mom and Dad didn't go to New York, either. The most important thing seemed to be for the five of them to spend the weekend together.

Sally called Jenny to tell her they weren't coming. "I can't believe it," Jenny said. "That's too ghastly. Jake and I had planned all these things. In two days,

141

we were going to do everything we did together last year in a whole month."

"Emily and I are sick about it," Sally said. "We're so disappointed, we can't stand it. But it's just one of those things. It can't be helped."

"I don't know how you can take it so calmly," Jenny said.

Because the beach just doesn't seem so important anymore, Sally thought. But what she said was, "I'm not calm, really. I just sound calm."

Tuesday morning, Sally and Emily didn't go to camp. They went to see Dr. Ghardelli instead. Lisa couldn't go; she had to work. She made them promise to write down everything Dr. Ghardelli said and show it to her later.

They sat down in the waiting room while Mom gave their names to the receptionist. It didn't look like a waiting room in a doctor's office; it looked like their grandmother's cheerful, overcrowded living room. The furniture was slipcovered in flowered chintz, the coffee table was piled high with magazines, shelves on the wall were loaded with books, and there was even a large tank filled with brilliant tropical fish.

The people surprised Sally, too. One man, thin and pale, came in leaning on a cane, but Sally couldn't tell whether he needed the cane because he had cancer or because he was simply very old. One woman was wearing a wig. Sally knew that chemotherapy caused some people to lose their hair, though this hadn't happened to her mother, and it hadn't happened to any of the other people in the waiting room, either. As a matter of fact, they looked just like the patients she saw in the dentist's waiting room. They were regular human beings. You certainly couldn't tell by looking at them that they had cancer. Maybe they thought she and Emily had cancer. Maybe they were sitting there thinking, Look at those two beautiful girls. Sisters, obviously, maybe even twins. So young, what a pity. . . .

Mom did go with them into Dr. Ghardelli's office, but she didn't say anything. She let Sally and Emily ask all the questions, of which they had plenty. When they finally ran out, Dr. Ghardelli told them to call her up anytime if they thought of more.

"Well?" Mom asked as they left the office.

"I'm still scared," Emily said. "But instead of being a lot scared, I'm just a little scared."

"Now at least if I'm cross and mean, I'll know why," Sally said. "Maybe knowing why will help."

"Yeah," Mom said. "Me, too."

She took them to Dunkin' Donuts for what was either a late breakfast or an early lunch, then dropped them off at Camp Totem. Sally arrived in time for drama. The Apaches were still working on their camp version of *Macbeth*.

"This is turning out to be pretty funny," Maxie said. "I still think we should do it for the powwow. I really do."

"We're doing the tepee," Angelo said. "I told you. You see, it'll be a race. We'll do it faster than the Senecas, and we'll win."

"We practiced twice already," Sally said, "and we're still not very good at it. The play is good."

"Hey, wait a minute," Claire interrupted. "This play has a long way to go before it's presentable."

"Well," Sally amended, "it'll get good. But the tepee raising will never get good."

"What is this?" Angelo asked. "A revolution?"

Sally answered his question with another. "Didn't you study American history in school?"

"Sure I did. That's where I learned about revolutions."

"Then you know it doesn't matter who you are—a king, a dictator, an emperor, a president, a chief—you're not going to last very long if all your people are against you. Like Macbeth."

"Oh, come on," Marty interrupted, "let's get back to the play. Where were we, guys? Oh, yeah, Macbeth is going to hire these two creeps to kill Banquo. Who wants to be the murderers? Maybe a couple of the witches."

"You can forget about me," Angelo said. "I'm not going to be in this stupid play."

"But you have to be in it," Melanie cried. "You're the lead. You're the star."

"Forget it," Angelo said. He glanced at Gerald. "If anyone's looking for me, I'll be in the crafts shop, working on my wallet." Then he turned away and stalked off down the hill.

"Hey, Gerald," Sally exclaimed, "you can't let him do that. We need him. The play will fall apart without him."

But Gerald made no effort to call Angelo back. "Anyone can play Macbeth," he said. "If Angelo doesn't want to be in the play, no one can make him."

Sally suspected that Angelo did want to be in the play. Maybe he just wanted them to show him some respect. But she wasn't sure how they could do that. To Angelo, respect seemed to mean agreeing with everything he said.

"We're not going to have anything ready for the powwow," Melanie said in a voice heavy with gloom. "We won't have a tepee or a play."

"Oh, who cares about the old powwow, anyway," said Maxie. "We're too old for dumb powwows."

"Maxie, you be Macbeth," Claire suggested.

Maxie collapsed on the ground. "Nah, I don't want to be."

"Angelo's right," Gil said. "This play is stupid." He fell to the ground as well. So did several of the others. The only ones remaining on their feet were Sally and Marty.

"Well," said Claire, "you can't do *Macbeth* with two people. Sally, Marty, you sit down, too, and I'll tell you a story."

"Hamlet," Sally suggested. She was certainly disappointed at the play's sudden collapse, but she was eager to hear about the man all in black who held a skull in his hand.

"Okay," Claire said. *"Hamlet."*

Long ago, Claire explained, Hamlet was the prince of Denmark. He was attending school in Germany when his father died. Hamlet, of course, hurried home for the funeral. Just a few days later, his mother, Gertrude, married his uncle Claudius, who then became the new king. Hamlet wasn't happy about that at all. He was even less happy about it when his father's ghost appeared on the castle walls one night and told him that he hadn't just died, he'd been murdered. The murderer was the dead king's own brother, Claudius, now his widow's husband! The ghost urged Hamlet to avenge his murder. "Remember me," he murmured as he faded away in the first light of dawn.

Hamlet wanted to avenge his father's murder. But what if the ghost was really a devil disguised as his father, a devil trying to lead Hamlet to his own destruction? Hamlet decided to act as if he were crazy in order to gain enough time to discover the truth.

The only one he told of his plan was his friend Horatio. His poor girlfriend, Ophelia, really believed he was crazy. Her father, Polonius, thought Hamlet was out of his mind with love. But shrewd King Claudius suspected the truth.

A company of traveling actors arrived at the castle to entertain the court. Hamlet told them to perform *The Murder of Gonzago,* a play in which a man kills his brother by pouring poison into his ear while he's sleeping, just the way Claudius had murdered Hamlet's father. "The play's the thing," Hamlet said, "wherein I'll catch the conscience of the king."

Claudius and Gertrude were very upset by the play and rushed out of the hall. Hamlet was sure he had Claudius now. He hurried to his mother's room, where he heard a rustling behind the curtains. He drew his sword and ran the intruder through. But it was not the king he killed. It was only Polonius, who had been spying on him.

Claudius sent Hamlet to England, to save him, he said, from the anger of the people over the death of Polonius. With Hamlet, Claudius sent sealed letters ordering the king of England to put Hamlet to death. But Hamlet opened the letters, and when pirates attacked his ship, he escaped back to Denmark.

Hamlet met Horatio in a graveyard, where a new grave was being dug. The grave diggers turned up the skull of Hamlet's childhood friend, the jester Yorick.

Hamlet picked up the skull and stared at it. "Alas! poor Yorick," he said. "I knew him, Horatio, a fellow of infinite jest."

When the funeral procession arrived, Hamlet realized the grave was Ophelia's. Truly crazed with grief over the loss of both Hamlet and her father, she had killed herself.

King Claudius persuaded Ophelia's brother, Laertes, that he could avenge the deaths of his father and sister by fighting a duel with Hamlet. The king poisoned the tip of Laertes's sword, so that even a minor prick would kill Hamlet. He also prepared a poisoned cup of wine as a backup. But during the fight, Hamlet and Laertes exchanged swords. They were both pricked with the poison. Before Claudius could stop her, Gertrude drank a toast to her son from the poisoned cup. Finally, just before he died, Hamlet managed to run Claudius through.

"At the end of the play," Claire said, "the stage is littered with bodies. The only one left alive is Horatio. Alone he welcomes Fortinbras, prince of Norway, who comes to restore order to Denmark and provide the noble Hamlet with an honorable burial. 'Good night, sweet prince,' Horatio says at the end, 'and flights of angels sing thee to thy rest!' "

"More blood and guts," Sally said when the story was over.

"Also the most powerful poetry ever written," Claire said. "That's why you have to read it for yourself one day."

"I can't understand the poetry," Sally said.

"You will, with the help of a good teacher."

"No one ever actually goes to see that play, do they?" Melanie asked. "The ending is too sad. It's not like Macbeth. You don't mind that Macbeth dies at the end, because by then he's really a bad guy. But Hamlet's a good guy all the way through."

"People have been flocking to see *Hamlet* for nearly four hundred years," Claire said. "Of course the ending is tragic, but that doesn't make the audience feel depressed. If the play's well done, it makes them feel uplifted—sort of cleansed inside and purified."

Sally shook her head. "I don't understand." She did feel sorry for Ophelia, though, so depressed by her losses that she'd actually killed herself.

"Well, you will understand someday, when you see a tragedy acted out on the stage or even in the movies," Claire said. "It just has to be well done to work, that's all."

Sally thought it would be a long time before she understood what Claire was talking about, if ever. Their version of *Macbeth* was an improvement on Shakespeare's, she thought, because it was funny, not sad. She really felt terrible that they'd abandoned it.

After supper, Lisa sat Emily and Sally down on the back porch to find out what Dr. Ghardelli had said. "Where are your notes?" she asked.

"We didn't take any," Emily admitted.

"But you promised. . . ."

"We were too busy listening," Sally explained.

"But we remember everything," Emily added.

"You don't," said Lisa.

"We do," Sally insisted. "A person always remembers what she thinks is really important."

"We'll see about that," Lisa said. "First of all, I want to know if Mom is going to die—I mean anytime soon—of cancer."

"Yeah, that was the first question we asked, too," Emily said. "The answer is probably not."

"*Probably* not?" Clearly, Lisa was not satisfied.

"All of Dr. Ghardelli's answers were like that," Sally explained. "It's all statistics. That's why she couldn't ever just say yes or no. She told us cancer kills more people in the United States today than any other illness except heart disease. But she also said you can get rid of it, especially if it's caught early."

"And Mom's was caught early," Emily said. "It hadn't spread."

"If it hasn't spread," Sally went on, "ninety-five percent of breast cancer patients have no disease five years later. After the chemo is over, Mom has a good chance of living as long as someone who never had cancer."

"Only they can't be sure," Emily added.

"I guess that will have to do," said Lisa. "What about the other big question? Will we get cancer?"

"Bad news and good news," Emily said. "The bad news is that daughters of women who've had breast cancer are three times more likely to get it than other women. The good news is that breast cancer doesn't kill you if it's found early and treated properly."

Sally crossed her arms over her chest and hugged her breasts. "This is the important thing. Mom's doctor found her cancer pretty early, but if Mom had found it earlier herself, before it got so big, maybe she would have just taken out the lump and had radiation, instead of chopping off the whole breast. We had to promise Dr. Ghardelli we'd examine our breasts every single month to see if we were growing any lumps. You have to do it, too."

Like Sally, Lisa hugged her chest. "Emily doesn't even have breasts. And yours are hardly noticeable. I guess I'm the one who has to worry."

"Yeah, just you," Emily agreed. "Kids hardly ever get breast cancer. Sally and I don't have to start that self-examination stuff until we menstruate. Then our doctor will show us how to do it, or Mom will. Or we can read a pamphlet from the American Cancer Society."

Lisa's arms dropped to her side. She leaned her head against the back of her chair. "I feel better," she said. "I don't know why; I just feel better. I mean, Dr. Ghardelli didn't say Mom for sure wasn't going to die of cancer. She didn't say for sure we weren't going to die of cancer. She didn't say for sure we weren't going to get it. All she did was give you a lot of numbers."

"In a nice tone of voice," said Sally.

"Well, I feel better, anyway. Do you?"

Emily nodded. "Definitely," Sally agreed. She wasn't even upset that the Apaches would have nothing to present at the powwow. Not much, anyway.

"The truth chases the monsters out of your head," Emily said. "It's like what you were imagining was so much worse than what's really going on."

"I'm tired," Sally said. "But it's a good kind of tired." She felt drained, yet at the same time relieved, relaxed. It was as if she'd gone through a whirlpool and survived. Maybe that was how people felt after they watched *Hamlet* on the stage. Maybe that was what Claire had been talking about.

T E N

"Well," Claire asked the next day, "are we going to do this play or aren't we?"

"The play is off, Claire," Maxie said. "You might as well forget it."

"We can do theater games, like the first few times you were with us," Melanie suggested. "They were fun."

"Not as much fun as *Macbeth*," Sally said. "We need Angelo back." They were sitting in front of the Apache tent; Angelo and Gil were several yards off, throwing stones at a tree. "Angelo was the soul of that play. He was made for the part." The reason the play had become so funny was that Angelo had taken it so seriously. "We have to find a way to get him to change his mind."

Maxie waved his hand dismissively. "We weren't even done working it out. We'd only gotten to the part where Macbeth goes to the witches' cave to ask for advice. How were we going to do that with gypsies? Gypsies don't hang out in caves. These gypsies were living in trailers."

Sally leaped to her feet as if she'd been struck by lightning. "I've got it!" she cried. "I've got it! They're not living in trailers. They're living in a tent. Actually, they're living in a tepee. And we'll put that teepee up before the play begins, right in front of everyone. So we can do both things—the tepee and the play." She plopped down next to Marty. "Go tell him that idea. Maybe he'll come back."

"Whose fault do you think it is that he's gone?" Marty asked.

"Well . . . his own, I guess," Sally said. "Or maybe it goes back to that fight you and he had."

"Whose fault was the fight? Who stood there yelling 'Get him, get him,' like a screaming hyena? Who made some mean remark about Angelo every time she had the chance?" Marty stared at her. "Who? Who?"

Sally stared back at him. "You mean me, don't you?"

"Yeah. I mean you."

"But why should Angelo care what I say? I'm nobody."

"Come off it, Sally," Marty returned. "People listen to you. You know it."

"Angelo's a bully," Sally said.

Marty made no reply.

"Sometimes," she amended. She thought back over the whole time she'd been at camp. She tried to remember every word she and Angelo had ever said to each other. Never anything nice that she could recall. Actually Angelo hadn't said much to her at all. He'd more or less left her alone. Suddenly the things she had said to him seemed somehow sharper, nastier than the things he had said to her. Maybe Angelo had been a bully, but what she had been was mean. "I guess I should apologize," she murmured.

"If you really want him back."

Slowly she rose to her feet. Slowly she walked toward the tree at which Angelo was flinging stones with such venom that she wouldn't have been surprised if he knocked it over. "Hey, Angelo," she called.

He didn't answer. She moved closer. "Angelo, we have an idea."

Still he didn't answer.

"Hey, Angelo," she added softly, "I want you to know I'm sorry. We need you. Come on back—please."

Then Angelo turned. If he hadn't been Angelo, Sally would have thought he'd been crying. "Why should I?" he said. "No one wants me. I got to be chief fair and square, but still no one wants me. That's not how it was last session."

"Well," Sally said, "now it's this session." She swallowed hard. "Just listen to our idea. It'll only take a minute. And then you'll just say yes or no. If you say no, I'll leave you alone."

Angelo didn't answer, but he didn't turn away, either.

Sally forced herself to continue. "The play fell apart without you. You were the star. We thought maybe you'd come back if we did what you wanted and built a tepee."

Angelo straightened. He fixed his large black eyes on her.

"But as part of the play. So we can do what we want, too," Sally added. Angelo slumped again. "That's fair," she continued quickly. "You have to admit that's fair. The gypsies will live in a tepee. And the first thing we'll do, before the play even starts, is put it up, right in front of everybody, faster than the Senecas. And then we'll use it, we'll do a play with it. You can bet the Senecas never thought of anything as good as that!"

"I guess not," Angelo responded grudgingly.

"So it's okay?" Sally queried eagerly. "You'll come back?"

"We could take a vote," Angelo suggested. He

seemed to be cheering up again. Apparently, he'd suddenly realized the truth. He couldn't lose.

Back at the tent, Claire managed the election. "Close your eyes, everyone," she said. They all obeyed, though Sally imagined several of them, like she herself, were peeking through their fingers. "If you want to do this play for the powwow, along with building a tepee, raise your hands . . . okay, it's unanimous."

Sally clapped her hands. She felt happy, totally happy, for the first time in three months. The Apaches were really a tribe at last. True, camp was almost over—but better now than never.

And it wasn't too late. They worked like beavers the next two days. Except for swimming, they did nothing but the play and the tepee, the tepee and the play. Claire couldn't be with them all the time, but they practiced by themselves. Cliff Breakwater helped them with the tepee part. He didn't say a word about the Senecas and their tepee. The Apaches still had lots of fights, but they managed to work their way through them, even when neither Claire nor Cliff was around. Gerald, as usual, was no help, but that didn't seem to matter so much anymore.

Mom and Grandma came to the powwow. Dad, Lisa, and Grandpa would have come, too, but they were working. First, there was an opening ceremony led by Cliff Breakwater. Each tribe marched down from its tent to the campfire area to the beat of Cliff's drum. The chief of each tribe marched first, carrying a burning torch. The chiefs lit the campfire; then all the tribes together sang the camp song.

> Far above Lake Totem's waters
> Stands the camp of many parts.
> No matter how far life may take us
> Camp Totem's mem'ry's in our hearts.

The words didn't make much sense to Sally, but when they all sang it so loud, she supposed no one noticed.

The baby tribes went first. The Seminoles sang two Indian songs and did dances to go with them. The Mohawks sang and danced, too. Both tribes were very large and very young. Sally supposed there wasn't much else they could do for a show.

The Utes performed next. They made everyone get up and walk through their tent to look at the Indian baskets, belts, and necklaces they'd woven from straw and leather.

The Pawnees enacted a buffalo hunt. The kids pretending to be buffaloes wore furry masks with horns. The others were dressed as Indians, with feathered headdresses and bead-trimmed pants and skirts. They

must have put hours into their costumes alone. "Pretty impressive," Marty whispered to Sally.

She agreed. "If it weren't for us, they'd win."

"Don't be so sure we're going to win," Maxie warned. "The judges may think we're just weird." Cliff Breakwater, Ruth, and Mr. Bernabe, who owned the camp, were the judges.

The Senecas demonstrated Indian sports. They got the whole audience up to play one game, which involved kicking a leather ball between two teams. It didn't matter how big the teams were. Coopy Palmer, the Seneca chief, explained that the Indians sometimes played this game with two hundred people on each side.

"Hey, Sally," Angelo said, "I thought you told us the Senecas were going to put up a tepee." He wasn't mad. He was happy that the only tepee at that powwow would be his. He just wanted to know what had happened.

Sally shook her head. She couldn't decide whether she was furious or merely amazed. "My sister lied to me," she said. "My twin sister. She deliberately threw me off the track."

"Well, you have to admit, this was different," Angelo said. "They got everyone into it. Maybe they'll win."

"Have we had fun with our play?" Sally asked sharply. "Have we?"

"I guess so," Angelo admitted.

"Well, that's what matters, isn't it?"

No one answered her. Having fun had been good enough yesterday, but now that they were actually in the powwow, they wanted to win.

And the play went very well, Sally thought. The Apaches were really into their parts, Angelo especially. The audience cheered when the tepee went up in five minutes flat, and then, during the show, they all laughed in the right places. The Apaches got a standing ovation when it was over. But then, so had the Pawnees and the Senecas.

While they were waiting for the judges' decision, Sally climbed up the bleachers to the spot where her mother and grandmother were sitting. Emily was already there. "Emily, you're a rat fink," Sally said. "You lied to me."

"We were going to build a tepee," Emily replied calmly. "We changed our minds later on."

"She didn't tell me, either," Mom said. "I didn't know what the Senecas were really doing until I saw it here today."

"We swore we wouldn't tell," Emily explained. "In blood."

"Oaths like that don't count for twins," Sally said.

"Did you ever tell me what the Apaches were doing?" Emily snapped. "So why did I have to tell you what the Senecas were doing? You didn't tell me much of anything this summer."

"Whose fault was that?" Sally retorted. "You didn't even want me in your tribe."

"Girls!" Mother interjected. "What's going on? I thought you two were friends again. At least, I hoped so."

"We're not friends," Emily said. "We're sisters."

"Sisters have to fight," Sally agreed. "It doesn't mean anything. Right, Em?"

"Right. Your play was funny. It was funnier than most stuff on TV."

"Your games were great," Sally returned. "That was the best idea I ever heard of."

Ruth, Cliff Breakwater, and Mr. Bernabe were making their way toward the campfire. "I think you'd better go back now," Grandma said. "It looks to me like they're getting ready to announce the winner."

Sally and Emily clambered down the bleachers. When they reached the bottom, they separated with a wave. Sally took her place between Marty and Melanie. "I'm so nervous," Melanie said as she grabbed Sally's hand and held it tightly.

Ruth, Cliff Breakwater, and Mr. Bernabe whispered together for another minute or two. Then Ruth stepped forward and held up her hand for silence. The response was total and immediate.

"This is my third year as head counselor at Camp

Totem," Ruth said. "Before that, I was a tribe counselor for three years. In six summers, I have never seen a powwow to equal this one. Every single tribe was so wonderful that Cliff, Mr. Bernabe, and I found it almost impossible to come to a decision." She paused and smiled.

"The usual junk," Maxie said.

"I didn't hear her say it last session," Angelo returned.

Ruth was speaking again. "To the Seminoles and the Mohawks, I want to say that each of you is completely deserving of the prize. If you weren't up against kids much older and more experienced than yourselves, you certainly would have won. I want the Seminoles and the Mohawks to stand up now." Crowds of little kids jumped to their feet. "Let's hear it for the Mohawks and the Seminoles." The other tribes and the visitors cheered wildly. The Mohawks and the Seminoles sat down again, apparently satisfied.

"To the Pawnees and the Utes," Ruth continued, "I want to say that in any other year your superb presentations would have won without a doubt, even against the older tribes. You are to be congratulated on your creativity, originality, and hard work." She made them stand up, too, and everyone cheered even harder than they had for the baby tribes. When they sat down, they seemed, if not quite as happy as the Mohawks and the Seminoles, happy enough.

Ruth walked toward the Senecas. When she reached them, she turned and faced the audience. "Ladies and gentlemen," she announced, "I give you the Senecas, winners of this year's Camp Totem trophy."

The Senecas leaped to their feet, screeching and hugging each other. They broke into their tribe cheer.

Who's the best
Of all the rest?
S—E—N
E—C—A
Yea!!!

The Seminoles, Mohawks, Utes, and Pawnees cheered, too. Sally and some of the other Apaches tried to applaud politely, but it wasn't easy. Sally had tears in her eyes, and she wasn't the only one. All her talk about fun being the most important thing had been, she realized, a lot of garbage. "Don't feel bad," Gerald was saying. "You were the best so far as I'm concerned." No one paid any attention to him.

Suddenly Angelo poked Marty. "Hey look," he said. "Ruth's coming over here." She stood in front of them, and once again there was silence.

Ruth turned. Now her back was to the Apaches, but they held on to every word coming out of her mouth as if it were gold.

"Ladies and gentlemen, please, I'm not through. I

wish to say something about the Apaches. They didn't win, but I don't mind telling you that the judges argued long and hard about whether the plaque should go to the Apaches or the Senecas. We all agreed that the Apache presentation was the most creative of all. However, we also felt that the Native American traditions of Camp Totem must be upheld. In spite of the tepee, we decided that the Apache presentation was more Shakespeare than Indian. That's why we finally settled on the Senecas. Both tribes were so terrific, it's not surprising that we struggled so hard over this decision. Cliff, Mr. Bernabe, and I want you to know that if there was a prize for the funniest and the most imaginative presentation, there's no doubt the Apaches would have won it."

Ruth turned and faced the tribe. "Congratulations to Claire and all the Apaches for an absolutely smashing contribution." And then, once again, she made everyone stand up and cheer. That cheer lasted the longest of all.

Afterward, campers, counselors, and guests ate watermelon and cookies. The Apaches ran around looking for one another in order to say good-bye. Kids hugged and kissed and promised to call during the winter, but their eyes didn't really look at you when they said it. Sally knew it wouldn't happen. Already camp was receding into the past, as if it had been over a long time ago, instead of just this afternoon.

In less than two weeks, school would start and camp would seem like something that had happened to someone else.

"We should have won, kiddo," Marty said as he gave her shoulder a farewell poke.

"Well, we almost won," Melanie said. "We did pretty good, and it was fun, like you said, Sally." An hour ago, winning had mattered so much. And now it didn't matter at all.

But there was one person to whom Sally had no intention of saying a permanent good-bye. She found Claire eating watermelon with a bunch of other counselors. She squatted on the ground next to her. "Don't forget, Claire, you still owe us a dinner."

"Let's take a little walk, Sally," Claire said. "I want to talk to you."

Sally stood up, Claire reached out her hand, and Sally helped her hoist herself to her feet. They started off up the hill, toward the Apache tent. "Did your family talk?" Claire asked.

"Oh, yes," Sally said. "Things are better in our house now. I should have told you that before, but we've all been so busy the last few days."

"Your mom and I bumped into each other at the watermelon table. She looks good, doesn't she?"

Sally nodded.

"Well, I told her what I'm going to tell you." Claire stopped walking, turned toward Sally, and put her arm around her. "Sally, I'm going back to California."

Sally felt as if a fist were grasping her heart. "What do you have to do that for?"

"I've been in my daughter's house long enough. She's going to get married again, you know."

"I didn't know."

"It's wonderful. She's so happy." Claire squeezed Sally's shoulder. "You see, honey, there is life after cancer."

"She's so happy that she's throwing you out?" Sally exclaimed bitterly.

"She's not throwing me out," Claire said. "Come on, try to understand."

Sally frowned. Grown-ups were always telling kids to understand. But did *they* ever try to understand?

Claire went right on talking. "You saw there was scarcely room in that apartment for four people, let alone five. And I want to go, Sally. All my friends are in Los Angeles. I'm pretty lonesome in New Jersey."

"What about me?" Sally retorted. "What about Emily?"

"I'm sixty and you're eleven," Claire said. "Everyone needs friends her own age. But you and Emily are certainly my friends, too, and I think you always will be. You did so much for me this summer."

"We did?"

Claire smiled. "You showed me what my life's work really is—at least my life's work for what's left of my life. I've got a job at a community center in Los Angeles teaching creative dramatics and I'm going to take some courses in it, so I can do it even better."

"Humph," Sally grunted. "That doesn't do us much good, does it?"

"Listen, silly, I'm not leaving tomorrow. There's plenty of time for souffles and more Shakespeare stories." Claire waggled her finger in front of Sally's nose. "And I have a great idea. The Shakespeare stories I don't get to tell you, I'll write to you. I'll put them in letters."

"That's a lot of work," Sally said. "They're long stories."

"Yes," Claire agreed, "but it'll be fun, too. *Claire's Tales from Shakespeare.* That sounds pretty good, don't you think?" She leaned over and kissed Sally's cheek. "You've changed my life, Sally. Thank you."

Sally knew that the same was true for her. And she knew that she'd better say so now, in case she never had another chance. "Well, thank you, too. Thank you for the Apache play. Thank you for understanding about cancer. Thank you for Shakespeare. Call us when we're supposed to come over."

She spoke so quickly, Claire had no chance to reply. And when she was finished, she ran down the hill as fast as her legs would carry her. Fat Claire couldn't possibly catch up.

Sally found Emily, her mother, and her grandmother waiting for her at the car. "Claire's going away," she announced.

"Yes," her mother replied. "She told me. I know you'll miss her. She's an interesting woman."

"She didn't tell me," Emily complained.

"Well, you'll see her," Sally said. "We're still going to go there for dinner. And she promised to write to us." Sally had no faith in the phone calls the other Apaches had promised, but she believed that Claire's promise was different. She really would send them Shakespeare stories in the mail, because it was something she really wanted to do.

"Girls, listen," Mom interrupted, "I've got something to tell you about tonight's dinner. We're going to meet Dad and Lisa at Renato's for pasta. And guess who else is going to be there?"

"Oh, come on, Mom, tell us," Emily begged. "Don't make us play games."

"What's tomorrow?" Mom asked.

"Saturday," Sally said.

"The last Saturday in August," Mom said. "Who comes home the last Saturday in August?"

"We always came home from the shore the last Saturday in August," Sally said. "When we went."

"Which means Jenny and Jake are coming home tomorrow," Emily added.

"Only they're not coming home tomorrow. To avoid the traffic, they came home today. So we're meeting Aunt Lou and Uncle Andrew and Jenny and Jake for supper, too!"

Sally let out a long sigh. "Super," she said. "That's super." She climbed into the backseat of the car. Emily climbed in next to her. Mom sat behind the wheel, the way she used to, with Grandma next to her. She started the car and inched it carefully out of the gravel parking lot and down the dirt road that led out of camp.

Sally leaned back in her seat. The summer was over. The Four Seasons—she, Emily, Jenny, and Jake— would start meeting again. Maybe they could put on a Shakespeare play for Mom's birthday. Sixth grade would begin. They'd need really smashing stuff for sixth grade. Mom would take them shopping.

Sally rolled down the window. The fresh wind that blew on her face was tinged with coolness. It smelled of autumn and new beginnings.

ABOUT THE AUTHOR

"I love to hear stories of other people's childhoods," says Barbara Cohen, "as I loved to listen to my relatives tell stories of their past when I was small. I started writing as soon as they taught me how to form letters."

Perhaps that is why all of Ms. Cohen's books, whether based on the Bible, on her own childhood experiences, or on stories her relatives told her, speak directly to the reader in the voice of an authentic storyteller—one who truly understands what it is like to be young. Her stories reflect a warm, realistic perception of the strengths, strains, and humor of family life.

Ms. Cohen has lived in New Jersey all her life. She taught high school English for eleven years and taught in college part time before devoting her full attention to writing books for young people. She has raised three daughters and is very active in her synagogue.